KENTUCKY BLUE BLOODS

BLUEGRASS REUNION SERIES - BOOK 2

JAN SCARBROUGH

SADDLE HORSE PRESS

Copyright © 2018 Jan Scarbrough
Scarbrough, Jan
Kentucky Blue Bloods
Media > Books > Fiction > Romance Novels
Category/Tags: romance, Kentucky Bluegrass, horses, blue-blooded, British

Print ISBN: 978-0-9971920-5-6
1st Print Release July 2018

Edited by Karen Block
Cover Design by The Killion Group Inc.

This edition is published by agreement with Saddle Horse Press, PO Box 221543, Louisville, KY 40252.

❀ Created with Vellum

*Kathy Bloom, wonderful touring partner and
sister-in-law*

INTRODUCTION

Regina Ward, granddaughter of Corbin Ward, breeder of multiple stakes winners, had blood as blue as anyone in Kentucky. But what her grandfather had built, her father had gambled away. He'd already lost four prized horses to an arrogant, infuriating Brit. Reggie isn't about to lose her heart to him as well.

Caretaker to his family's thoroughbred racing empire, Parker Stuart has zero tolerance for anyone who slights him or his blue-blooded British family. Reggie may have considered their brief, torrid affair no more than a spring fling, but she'd run off with Parker's heart when she'd dumped him. Now it's time to settle the score.

It's up to Reggie to save what's left of her family homestead and her proud Kentucky heritage. But when Parker shows up to collect his horses, all bets are off. Reggie's never been a gambler and Parker despises losing. But when Kentucky blue blood tangles with British blue blood, are they willing to take a gamble on love?

Bluegrass Reunion Series: contemporary romances about second chances set in the Bluegrass of Kentucky that can be read as standalone novels with happily ever after endings and no cliffhangers.

CHAPTER ONE

Early September
Bourbon County, Kentucky

Bloody hell?

Parker Stuart cast a disbelieving gaze at the woman who'd met him at the airport. What was he, the youngest son of a proud British, thoroughbred-racing family, doing in a mud-caked pickup truck sitting beside a woman who resembled a caricature of a mountain hillbilly? His chauffeur certainly looked nothing like the young woman he remembered from London—the woman he'd flown across the Atlantic to seduce—again.

Women didn't dump him without regretting it.

Especially not the woman he'd fallen in love with and planned to marry.

Revenge wasn't a pretty sentiment, but it was just what he had in mind.

Love her and leave her. Like she'd left him. But he'd take four of her prized thoroughbreds home with him.

He should have known he was making a mistake, but three weeks spent in a haze of good sex—her body naked, writhing beneath him, driving him wild with desire—had fogged his brain. He had fallen in love, succumbing to an emotion he'd avoided for twenty-nine years.

Too bad she hadn't stuck around after their short fling. In fact, she had run out on him, leaving him sitting in the restaurant for nearly an hour, engagement ring in his pocket, before he'd finally checked his text messages. There'd been nothing sweet about her "dear John" goodbye.

For God's sake, she'd dumped him in a text!

No, the woman driving this bloody pickup looked nothing like the charming woman he'd met in London in the spring. That woman had possessed a quiet assurance and natural reserve. She'd had a genuine sweetness about her and a timeless beauty. Dressed in a classically feminine, floral-print cotton dress, she had worn a wide-brimmed, Southern Belle hat on her thick, blonde hair when he'd taken her to Ascot in June. She'd called it her "Derby" hat but had meant her derby, the one in Kentucky. Her American accent with its lovable Southern drawl charmed him, but most of all, he'd fallen in love with her shy, sensitive eyes, ones he couldn't forget.

Eyes now hidden by dark sunglasses.

Parker looked away. The central Kentucky countryside whizzed past, but he hardly saw it.

Granted, the moment he stepped off the jet at the airfield in Lexington, he had admired her curvy figure, fully appreciating those long shapely, and tanned legs. Yet, there was something objectionable about her dress, or lack thereof. She was wearing short, blue jean cutoffs with frayed cuffs, a skimpy white tank top that left nothing to his more than vivid imagination, and ankle-length barn boots—clunky, muddy, lace-up boots that smelled as if they'd tramped around a stable only minutes before his arrival.

Her apparel was an affront to him. To their time together. More than any burst of anger or recrimination, it told him exactly what to expect from this trip. She was thumbing her nose at him with her improper dress. She'd played him. He'd been a fool.

Not any longer.

Regina Ward, granddaughter of Corbin Ward, breeder of multiple stakes winners, had blood as blue as anyone in Kentucky but not as blue as his aristocratic British blood. Tainted only by the introduction of an American grandmother, Parker's blue-blooded family was heir to the fabled, Stuart racing stable, acres of prime London real estate, a historic estate in Kent, and a hereditary peerage granted to an ancestor by a reigning monarch five generations earlier.

No, this hayseed couldn't hold a candle to him. Her family was nothing. Her breeding operation was negligible. And he was going to drive a stake into the last of it.

Three years ago, Reggie's drunken father had beaten Parker's older brother in a game of poker, winning one of the Stuart's prize stallions. Now, the stallion, Stuart's Legacy, was dead after only three years in Kentucky. Although any horse could die from colic, Legacy's death was another mark against Reggie and her smalltime horse breeder father, Sam Ward.

Parker blinked hard. Focus. Don't let her get to you.

The countryside was not as lush and green as his homeland. He knew the Maury silt loam, with its underlying limestone base, made the soil perfect for raising horses. But thanks to the summer heat, the nutrient-rich grass looked dry. Inhospitable. Just like his welcome to the Bluegrass State.

Barreling down a Kentucky back road, flanked by black or white wooden fences and an occasional stone wall built by Scotch-Irish settlers, with a mad woman behind the wheel, who he barely recognized, didn't set right with Parker. Was he taking his life in his hands by being there?

He glanced again at Reggie.

"Does everyone in Kentucky drive this fast?" Parker added a touch of upper-class disdain to his voice.

She glanced at him and grinned, gum popping in her mouth. "Until we get caught."

He lifted an eyebrow. God, he hated women chewing gum. That more than anything put him off. She must have recognized his distaste, for she grinned and smacked her gum louder.

Parker cleared his throat. "How far is it to your farm?"

She flicked the turn signal and spun the steering wheel right, throwing him against the passenger side door.

"We're here," she said and popped her gum once more for good measure.

They bounced down a poorly-paved country lane bordered by tall oak trees, up a gentle knoll, pulled around a circular drive, and halted in front of a stately, Greek Revival house.

"Welcome to Richlawn Hall, built in 1830," she said with a touch of pride then opened her door and left him sitting alone in the cab.

Heat and humidity sucked the air from his lungs the minute he climbed from the truck. Parker put his hands on the small of his back and arched, stretching his cramped muscles.

Reggie came around the front of the truck and saw him. He couldn't read her eyes behind her sunglasses, but he had her attention. He played to his audience, prolonging his stretch, and thought her gaze may have been fixed on the button fly of his classic Paul Smith jeans.

"Our house is on the historic register," she informed him with an impish toss of her fifties-era ponytail.

"So is mine," he came back then perversely added, "several of them."

She fisted her hands at that. In the glare of the hot sun, standing in front of him, legs spread, hands on hips, she looked smug and self-assured, almost as if she was ready to do battle with an opponent. Him.

Brilliant! No matter how she tried to put him off with her gum popping and hillbilly attire, he was ready to take on this woman. Parker set his jaw and returned her stare.

Miss Regina Ward had no clue he was about to even the score —and enjoy himself wholeheartedly while doing it.

Reggie curled her fingers into fists, squeezing them so tightly her nails bit into her palms. She pressed her fists into her hips and squinted at the sun. She was angry—at herself, her father, and Mr. High-and-Mighty British Aristocrat, who was trying to ruin her life.

Look at him, standing there so proud and arrogant.

His hair was as black as she remembered and his eyes as deep blue. The tiny cleft in his chin and his high cheekbones gave him a noble look befitting his highfalutin' station. She smiled at him, recognizing hers wouldn't be a pleasant smile, and he glared back, as if not knowing what to think about her.

Reggie deepened her wicked smile and flipped her ponytail. Mr. High-and-Mighty, so confident in his fancy Armani suit coat, open-collar, white shirt and blue jeans, was about to get a rude awakening. Even in early September, Kentucky could be sweltering and oppressive. He'd soon learn it was foolhardy to wear such attire, especially on a working horse farm.

She chomped her gum. Oh, she was mad. Her father Sam had gone over the top this time. When he had won the older stallion, Stuart's Legacy, from Parker's brother Hampton, Sam had vowed it was the end of his poker playing. Damn! She'd been so naively happy, believing him again. Fat chance her dad could keep a promise. Now, his drinking and poker playing had turned into another freaking nightmare.

Legacy's successful stud career in Kentucky had revitalized the family breeding business that the death of her grandfather, more than three years ago, had nearly doomed. Sam wasn't a businessman—hell, he wasn't even much of a father—but Stuart's Legacy had been an unexpected godsend. It had come because of Sam's gambling addiction, but that didn't make it any less sweet.

Until Legacy colicked and died in June when she and her dad were in England.

Their farm manager, Ben, had tried to save Legacy, rushing the horse to Rood & Riddle Equine Hospital for surgery. But there had been complications. Nothing had hit Reggie as hard as losing that wonderful stallion, except the loss of her grandfather, who had been the steady rock in her life for over twenty years.

Mentally, Reggie shook her head. She was glad her sunglasses hid her eyes. She didn't want to reveal anything to Park—neither her thoughts about her family nor any stray feelings for him she'd not yet successfully squashed.

It had been one torrid affair in June. At the time, she'd never wanted it to end. Anger swelled at the memory. She'd had no business getting involved intimately with Park. The man was a love-"em-and-leave-'em type, too dangerous to surrender her heart to. She'd been totally out of her league and too damned scared she was losing control. When she realized what was happening, she'd fled from him for her own safety. Legacy's death had been the excuse she'd used to cover her panic.

"Is this *it*?" Park asked finally, his gaze sweeping the hall, a prime example of early Greek Revival architecture, to focus on the lone horse barn to its left. Pivoting, he surveyed the paddocks and fields, sloping downward away from them, original stone outbuildings, farm ponds, and mature shade trees.

"Sure this is *it*," Reggie snapped. "Did you think you were coming to some well-heeled horse farm?"

He took a step toward her, and she caught her breath. *Careful or he'll suck the resolve right out of your body.*

"I didn't know what to expect," he said in his high class British accent.

She clenched her teeth, refusing to admit her father had gambled away the bulk of the Ward estates. The yearling farm and the stallion farm were both gone in the years since Granddaddy had died. Only the broodmare farm remained, and luckily, Sam couldn't get his grubby paws on it. This farm was hers. Granddaddy had left it to her. To her alone.

And it was up to her to save it. *And* the Ward legacy.

"Would you like to step into the house?" she asked in a singsong voice, mocking his accent. "I'm sure you'd like to freshen up from your long journey."

"No, I find I'm remarkably fresh. Something about being here with you exhilarates me." He stopped inches away from her and looked down his regal nose at her.

She held her breath. Was he going to say something more? Something personal. Like "where were you that day? Why did you leave without saying goodbye in person? I've missed you."

Instead he dismissed her with a sharp glance and walked around her. "I'd like to see my horses."

Reggie gritted her teeth. "We board our yearlings at another farm. We've consigned them. They're being prepped for the September sale. I'll take you to see them tomorrow."

"Fine." He continued, not looking back. "I want to see what horses you do have."

"Okay, then." His imperious attitude angered her. He didn't own this farm, and he had no right to demand to see her horses. She glared at him, deciding to show him the breeding stock.

"Come with me." Reggie lengthened her stride and passed him, leading the way along a gravel road to the barn.

All was dark and quiet inside except for the gentle snuffling of horses in their stalls and birds twittering in the rafters. As always, the smells of straw and horseflesh assailed her senses, filling her with a feeling of comfort where there was seemingly none to be had at the moment. She swallowed hard, almost ingesting her chewing gum.

"These are mares," Park said, "and a few foals old enough to be weaned.

She turned, removing her sunglasses for the first time. "Of course, they are. This is a mare barn. We keep the horses inside during the heat of the day. The mares have been confirmed in foal again, most to Stuart's Legacy. We had a hundred percent live foal rate this year. That's almost unheard of."

He walked along the row of stalls, examining the index cards taped to each door that contained the pedigree of the foal inside. He glanced back at her with a quizzical look in his eyes, and she bristled. "We don't wean the foals until after the September sale, Park."

She didn't explain that they couldn't afford to wean the foals, not now. Lacking the land that had once been used for their yearling operation, there just wasn't enough space here to separate all the mares from their babies out of earshot. Weaning was stressful enough on both the mare and foal. It broke the emotional and nutritional bonds between the two which were started at birth.

It took hard earned cash to board her yearlings now. Reggie had to sell those horses to make money to pay another farm for the care of the weanlings.

"Why do you insist on calling me Park?" he asked behind a dark scowl. "My name is Parker."

She swished her ponytail. "You don't seem like a Parker. It's too damn formal. Whether you know it or not, you're more of a Park."

"You know me so flipping well."

She grinned at his snarky reply. Good. She really was getting under his skin.

Reggie walked two stalls away then turned to face him. What could she say? In England, she had thought she was beginning to know him and knowing him had scared the hell out of her. Now, she dogpaddled in deep water where her emotions were concerned. She didn't want to find him attractive. And sexy. Not again.

She looked him up and down. "I figure I knew you pretty well...for a time, that is."

A snarl literally escaped his lips. He apparently understood her reference to their lovemaking. Park closed the gap between them. He caught her chin in one hand, squeezing it so hard it hurt. She fought a grimace. Eyes sparking, his gaze bore into her.

"What game are you playing, Reggie?"

She shook free of his grip and stepped back. "Game? I don't know what you mean."

"Don't you?" His gaze raked over her, his eyes consuming all the bare flesh she'd intentionally left exposed for him to see. "Your outfit. Your behavior. This place."

"What's the matter with the way I dress? This is Kentucky, not a snobby, society polo match or some fancy box at Ascot. And as for my behavior, it's not every day my livelihood is stolen from me."

He smiled then; an evil, arrogant smile that raised Reggie's hackles even more.

"I'm not stealing anything from you. I have the bills of sale signed by your father for four thoroughbreds of my choosing. The papers are in my briefcase in the back of that damned lorry you drive."

"What? You don't carry them strapped to your person? I'd think such important documents were worth protecting."

"I can understand your anger," his tone softened before his eyes flashed full of his own resentment. "I was angry three years ago when your father stole Legacy from us."

He meant more by his words. He was referring to their affair. He was talking about the way she'd left him. Fine. Let him be angry. So was she.

"Nobody twisted your brother's arm. My father didn't hold a gun to his head."

"Things all work out for the best in the end, don't they?"

"For you, maybe," she snapped. "People with money—like you —seem to get everything they want."

He directed a very pointed gaze her way. "Money isn't everything."

Her heart skipped a beat. She paused, swallowing hard. Now, she was sure he was talking about them.

"When you've got it," she spat as anger, hurt and fear welled up inside of her all at once. She turned from him and strode down the aisle of the barn.

He followed her. She heard the soft scuffing of his fancy shoes on the rough asphalt floor. When she left the stable, she took a deep breath. This was her farm. Park might take a few horses—by rights, her father could gamble those away—but nobody was touching this land.

Reggie sensed Park's presence behind her. She turned. Silhouetted against the open barn door, the sunlight streaming around him, Park was a tall, imposing man, broad of shoulder, but with the touch of elegant grace that had attracted her to him last summer. Taking a step toward her, he ran his hands along her bare arms, grasped them and drew her to him. Reggie stared up at him. Inside, she melted, filled with memories, but she couldn't let him see her weakness.

She put her sunglasses back on.

"I haven't won all I want to win," he said quietly. "I don't like to lose, Reggie. You knew that when you left me."

"I don't like to lose either, Park," she said, deliberately calling him by the name that annoyed him. "Taking those horses will make it hard for me to make ends meet. But this is my home. I'll fight you or anyone who tries to take it away."

His grin was challenging. "Brilliant! I always enjoy a good fight."

CHAPTER TWO

He'd made a mistake touching her.

Parker knew it the moment he felt Reggie's smooth skin. He dropped his hands from her arms. Suddenly, jet lag caught up with him. He needed time to harness his emotions. Her leaving had gutted him. He'd been devastated. If he was going to exact the revenge he wanted, he needed a cool head. And patience. She must come to him. Crawl to him. Then he would laugh in her face and fly home without her, taking her yearlings with him.

Bloody good plan. It rushed through his head as the sun beat down upon him causing sweat to glaze his forehead.

"I'm okay with that freshening up now," he said quietly.

She looked at him with distrust at his change in tone. "Sure. Come with me."

"My pleasure."

She spun on her heel and strode away. He hung back, eyeing her fit bum and the tantalizing flesh that peaked from under frayed cutoffs that were much too short. His mother would be appalled if she saw Reggie like this. But no worries. He wouldn't bring Reggie home this time.

Memories of their lovemaking flashed through his mind. He

couldn't stop them. Couldn't put them aside, no matter how his brain spun with his plans for revenge. God, he was up for it.

This was Reggie. And he had loved her. Much too much and much too quickly. Seeing her now in her own environment confused him. Strained his nerves. He needed time to regain his resolve.

The sway of her hips as he followed her to the house didn't help. He hauled his leather rolling bag and canvas shoulder bag from the bed of the pickup truck and joined her at the entrance where she stood waiting, one of those cute hips jutting to the side, her hand on the opposite one.

"Whatsa' matter? Not used to carrying your own luggage?"

He grinned. Why did she hide her eyes behind those damn glasses? "I carry them all the time. What I'm not used to is seeing you, and so much of you, at that."

She stuck out her tongue and tossed her ponytail as she turned away from him and opened the massive front door with its six-pane transom.

Parker walked up the short step to the porch. Fluted, two-story Ionic columns, carved of wood, supported the portico over the main entry. The house's Greek Revival architecture was remarkably intact although shabby. The woodwork needed a fresh coat of white paint, especially the classical moldings that extended around the house and the clapboard siding itself. He had an eye for art, and not just the feminine kind. The house had seen better days but was brilliant in its own way.

The main entrance led into a soaring front hall. It also needed freshening up. The yellow paint on the doors and trim had faded. A graceful stairway that looked to be made of cherry wood had a banister with scroll-design stringers. It ascended to a landing then up to the second floor above them. Doors led into the living room and dining room, and another opened directly from the rear of the hall into what appeared to be a screened porch.

"The floors are the original white ash," Reggie said when she noticed him surveying the wooden floor.

She had removed her sunglasses, and he caught a quick look of concern. Was she worried what he thought of her home?

"Are you going to show me to my room?" His question was curt, accompanied by a gaze that lingered a little longer than was polite on the strawberry cream cleavage exposed by her skimpy tank top.

She squared her shoulders when she noticed the direction of his gaze and flushed a delightful shade of red.

"Upstairs, at the top of the front stairway, you'll find the north bedroom," she said. "I'll be in the kitchen, if you want something to eat."

He wasn't hungry and longed for nothing more than a hot shower and bed, but Parker wasn't going to miss any opportunity to be with his newly-rediscovered hillbilly opponent.

The room was where Reggie said—at the top of the stairs, the door open and inviting. But it was papered in a god-awful mustard-yellow and avocado-green floral print. A wool rug of another floral print covered the ash floor. A cherry wood, four-poster bed draped with a white quilted coverlet stood in the middle of the room. The narrow bed had room enough for only one person. So much for his seduction plans—at least in this bed.

Then again, a small bed might have its usefulness.

Sunlight streamed through four windows on the east and west walls. A fireplace with a plain white, wooden mantle centered the third wall.

He deposited his luggage in a large built-in closet. After shrugging off his jacket, he rolled up his sleeves and went downstairs.

The smell of perking coffee and frying bacon drew him to the kitchen. The room appeared to have retained its original woodwork, mantelpiece, and white ash floors, but it also looked completely renovated. It was the most modern of any room he'd yet seen in the house. The appliances were large and American-styled stainless steel. There were granite-topped counters, a big kitchen island, and cherry wood cabinets.

Reggie was standing at the stove with her back to him. She'd removed her boots and was barefoot. Damn! How was he going to retain his sanity when she presented that cute bum and long, shapely legs to his view? This week in Kentucky was going to be tough.

Maybe tougher than he'd imagined.

Park was in the room.

Reggie felt his presence with a sixth-sense magnified by the instant energy suddenly filling the kitchen. She didn't turn around. Fear gripped her. But she wouldn't show it. She couldn't afford to show it...or any weakness. The Brit was too compelling. Too damn sexy and unforgettable. Somehow, she had to make it through this week. Somehow, she had to make the best of a very bad situation.

"I hope you don't mind breakfast food," she said without glancing over her shoulder. It was a little after seven o'clock in the evening.

"Smells good."

He'd crossed the floor. She sensed him nearer. Almost feel his breath on the nape of her neck. Her skin prickled with awareness.

"It was the easiest to fix," she remarked casually.

Reggie didn't mention breakfast was all she knew how to cook. Domestic chores weren't her strong suit. She turned to face him, spatula in hand. He wasn't really that close—standing on the other side of the island. There was a span of granite-topped hardwood separating them. It was just his presence in the room unnerving her.

Why did the guy have to look so good in a rumpled white dress shirt with rolled up sleeves? Reggie shoved down her awareness of him and clung to her anger.

She wore a full-length apron, tied at the neck over her tank top, knowing it covered what Park enjoyed seeing. What a stupid idea it had been to wear the scanty top and cutoffs. She'd found his ogling unsettling, reminding her too much of June. At least, she felt more comfortable hiding behind a blue denim apron. Lesson learned. She'd stick to khakis and knit shirts from now on.

"There's coffee in the coffee maker on the counter." She nodded to her right. "I set out half-and-half and sugar. Or do you take artificial sweetener?"

A horrified look crossed his face. "I'm dismayed you don't recall."

Reggie jutted out her jaw. "Well, I don't. So help yourself to whichever you prefer."

Turning her back to him again, she lifted the crisp strips of bacon from the frying pan and put them on a paper towel to drain. From the corner of her eye, she spotted him pouring coffee into a mug. He poured in the creamer and took a sip, gazing at her over the rim of the mug.

She dropped bread into the toaster then began to scramble eggs, attempting to ignore Park. Damned hard to do, but she gave it the old college try. By sheer force of will, she steadied her hands. When everything was ready, she put it on a tray then turned to glare at him.

"Care to help?"

"My pleasure."

"Fine. I thought you might be too good to lift a hand."

He grinned and raised an eyebrow. Why did it feel like he was laughing at her? Maybe because he was. Terrific!

She nodded at the tray of food then picked up her own mug of coffee and a glass pitcher of orange juice. At least, she wasn't serving the juice straight from the carton. She did have a little class.

"Follow me."

She led the way to the house's southern porch just off the kitchen. The screened porch wrapped around one side of the L-shaped house and served as a breakfast nook and a sitting room with rocking chairs. Double doors led into the side yard and adjoining meadow.

Park placed the tray on the round table she'd set earlier with her grandmother's blue, quilted placemats and Bachelor Button patterned dinnerware from Louisville Stoneware. They were everyday dishes but suited her fine. She wasn't about to put on airs for her hoity–toity guest. The fact she'd set out placemats and the better stainless steel flatware was good enough.

Parker pulled out a chair for Reggie. It was solid wood, of high quality, with a rush seat. She eyed him, and he bowed slightly. Frowning, she collapsed into the seat without removing her apron. He scooted her forward then took the chair beside her.

The back of the house was as comfortable as the front was formal. The one-story, screened porch was surprisingly pleasant, being shaded by big oak trees and cooled by ceiling fans. The humidity didn't seem as oppressive here as it did outside in the sun.

Reggie offered him the various platters of food, and he filled his blue-flowered plate with eggs, bacon, fried potatoes, and almost burnt toast.

"I find I'm ravenous after all," he said and took a bite of bacon.

She glanced at him but didn't comment, digging into her own

food. She had a healthy appetite, which he remembered from their few weeks together in the spring. Parker watched her carefully, though surreptitiously.

Strands of blond hair escaped from her ponytail to frame her tanned face. She kept her head down, allowing her eyelashes, devoid of mascara, to shade her eyes. He noticed smudges on the thin skin under her eyes. Those hadn't been there in London. What had her worried? Was it the loss of her horses? Or his arrival?

Silence enveloped them. It was awkward. Uncomfortable. Lingering.

"I'm curious," he said, breaking the deadlock first.

She glanced up from her plate, laid down her fork, and wiped her mouth with a paper napkin. "About what?"

"Is bluegrass really blue?"

The look she gave him said he'd grown two heads.

"What?" he questioned her incredulity. "I'm serious. I've wondered about it for years."

"Well, sure it is, if you don't cut it," she said. "When you see meadows of seeding bluegrass waving in the June breeze, it appears blue. The blades of grass are not blue, just the flowers and seeds."

"Well, that clears up the mystery then."

Picking up her fork, Reggie huffed. "You're just pulling my leg."

"A fine leg it would be to pull."

"Stop it! I may have to put up with you for a week, but I don't have to like it. And I don't have to put up with your stupid attempts at flirting. Being a jerk doesn't become you."

"But it's fine for you to play one? Forgive me if I don't know the rules you Yanks play by. I was asking a simple question not trying to chat you up."

The cause of the argument lay like a bale of moldy hay between them. He wasn't going to broach it, and she was avoiding it, too. She'd left him. Played him for a fool. She knew it and knew he knew it.

"Sorry. My bad." She ducked her head and shoveled in a forkful of potatoes.

"I'd like to ask you about your yearlings, or will I be chastised for that kind of curiosity?"

She picked up her coffee mug and took a sip. "What do you want to know?"

"Something about them. Your impressions. Recommendations."

"You think I'm going to recommend which yearlings you should take? I'm not that stupid."

"We enjoyed our discussions about thoroughbred bloodlines in the past. You've got a good grounding. I came to respect your point of view."

Had he confounded her with his compliment? A telltale blush suggested he had. Parker continued, "You know I've done my homework."

"Yes, I'd guess you have." She sounded disheartened.

"Then tell me about your operation here. What has the Ward breeding farm become since the death of its patriarch, Corbin?"

"Stuart's Legacy is what happened, and you should know that." She set her fork down again and put her arms on the table as if to give her support. "The stallion had speed, matured early, and could go the classic distances. Those were qualities Corbin wanted in his horses."

"Qualities my father favors as well," Parker commented. "You no longer race your homebreds." His kept his statement light but actually wanted to know why the Ward family no longer ran their own horses.

"That's because my grandfather mandated in his will that we sell all the horses we raise," Reggie said and stood to clear the table.

The clouds in her eyes and pinched expression on her face told Parker her grandfather's death still affected her. He'd been dead three years. In those years, the Ward Farms had dwindled and their presence in the industry lessened. Selling off their stock obviously wasn't helping. It was almost a shame to be out to cripple them even more.

He couldn't go bloody soft now. This was business and payback.

The Wards had had the use of the Stuart's best bloody stallion for three years, and now Parker was going to recoup what he could.

"I guess I'll go to my room and study my notes for tomorrow," Parker said, when it became obvious conversation had ended. He stood too and followed her into the kitchen, carrying his dishes. "Do you need my help?"

"No," she responded curtly.

He turned toward the dining room, the way he'd entered the kitchen.

"Not that way." Reggie opened a door on the side wall and pointed. "This way."

He followed her direction. An enclosed, back stairway led conveniently from the kitchen up to the second floor of the house. Pausing in the doorway, he gazed down at her. Unspoken emotions flew between them. Shadows of sadness and loss were in her eyes. How would he feel if he'd been forced to surrender his thoroughbreds? He stifled an impulse to reach for her.

To hell with feelings of compassion. Parker clung to his anger. It was safer that way.

"Good night," he bit out.

Her jaw clenched. Her eyes burned into his. As he climbed the stairs, he felt as if a dagger was poised to strike his exposed back.

CHAPTER THREE

Five o'clock came mighty early, even more so in summer when it grew light by five-thirty, especially when Reggie had spent the night tossing and turning. Struggling out of bed at her usual time, Reggie didn't bother to shower. She'd taken one the night before, and so had Park. She'd heard the water running in the guest bathroom adjoining his room. After that, the light showing under his door had burned another hour then flicked off.

Why in the heck had she stayed up and waited? Had she thought he'd come out and draw her into his arms? Had she been hoping for it? She'd curled up on the cushioned loveseat in the small sitting area on the second floor landing, hugging her knees. Then, stilling her racing heartbeat and quieting her breathing, she'd thought back on the day. On the past three months. On her life.

After Granddaddy had died, things had gone so terribly wrong. Her father's arrogant and drunken belief in his card-playing abilities had paid off but only once. The arrival of Stuart's Legacy had given the farm a much needed shot in the arm. They didn't need to pay breeding fees any longer because they had their own stallion. Legacy had also garnered a decent fee from other breeders, who wanted to infuse their American bloodlines with a successful European line. But her father's gambling had lost them valuable property. Now, it had caused them to lose important stock and the money four yearlings would have brought at auction.

Reggie's personal life was in no better shape than the mess at the farm. She constantly struggled with her insecurities and demons. Learning to survive as a kid had meant hiding her feelings. It had also meant trying to be perfect, which had never been good enough for her father. She'd been perfect in Granddaddy's eyes. But her life had been filled with chaos after her mother's death. Her father would take her from the family farm, and they'd live together in Las Vegas or Atlantic City, just long enough for him to get tired of her. Then he'd drop her back at the farm. Back where sanity existed. And love. And sometimes a little bit of laughter.

She'd hid her anxiety pretty well, hadn't she? No one knew inside she was emotionally ten years old and feared expressing sentiments that could so easily be criticized and put down.

Wound tightly, she was in control. That was how she'd played the game. That's how she'd survived. The arrival of Park had thrown her into an emotional meltdown of sorts. Now, controlling her feelings was a constant battle.

When Park's light had gone out, she'd crept into her room and showered. Afterwards, she'd dropped like a brick into bed, but she hadn't gone to sleep. And now, it was time to get up and start her day all over again.

Reggie wasn't about to make yesterday's mistake when she'd been trying to antagonize Park with cutoffs and a tank top. Today, common sense prevailed, and she intended to cover her body from the prying eyes of the aristocrat who had tormented her sleep, or lack thereof. She found the last clean pair of khaki slacks in her closet and put them on. She slipped into a forest green, polo-style shirt—she had about twenty of the same kind—embroidered with the Ward Farm logo. She laced up her work boots, the same grubby ones she'd worn the previous day.

The coffeepot in the kitchen automatically came on at five o'clock. It was ready for Reggie when she arrived downstairs. She poured the hot brew into her well-worn mug, purchased from a national chain, peeled an overripe banana then chewed it slowly, one bite at a time.

Her mother had liked bananas. In the end, that was one thing she'd eat—Reggie's squashed banana sandwiches, only Reggie had pronounced it "skwushed." The sandwiches were simple enough for a ten-year-old to make. Scoop the peanut butter into a bowl, add a banana, mash the two together then spread the goo onto a slice of bread. Top it with another, and cut the sandwich into two pieces.

Reggie would sit by her mother's side and watch her eat, proud she could do something for her mom. Because there wasn't much anyone could do. Not with advanced-stage breast cancer. Not after the surgery, the chemo, and the radiation had failed to stop the disease. Sam hadn't handled it well, but he hadn't handled much of anything well for years. Always a boozer, he'd only drank more, distanced himself from Reggie and her mother, and took up playing poker. Thank God for her granddaddy. Corbin had stood by her and watched after Reggie's mom until the day she'd died upstairs in the home where they'd lived at the time.

"Take care of your daddy," her mother had said. "He's a weak man. He doesn't have your strength."

A ten-year-old with strength? Reggie hadn't felt very strong. She'd felt scared and helpless. Her father hadn't been there, and it had made her angry. Before the end, Reggie had given her promise to her mother. Then her grandfather had taken her away.

Reggie had tried to take care of her father. But Sam was an impossible case. And, deep down, she'd never forgiven him for not being there for her. And now, he'd betrayed her again. She didn't know how she'd survive the loss of the four horses.

Shaking away her non-productive funk, Reggie went outside to work.

In the twenty-stall barn near the house, Ben, her farm manager, and Juan, her all-around handyman, were already cleaning the empty stalls. Acknowledging them with a terse nod—it was morning, after all, and no one with any sense talked until after nine o'clock—Reggie picked a filthy stall and slid open the door. With a stall fork, she shoveled manure into the spreader attached to a tractor in the wide aisle, then bedded the stall with clean shavings. Going to the next stall, she repeated the process—shovel, lift, sift, toss.

Her grandfather used to say the recurring nature of the business was something you had to love. Just as you had to love animals and working with them. You had to love being outdoors in all kinds of weather or else the horse business killed you. It was hard work, and the ups and downs had the potential to destroy your soul. Triumphs were few and far between, but you lived for the dream of raising the next Kentucky Derby winner, the next Triple Crown champion.

Ben poked his head inside the stall. "How'd it go yesterday?"

Reggie rested her arm on the handle of her fork and took a deep breath. Ben Johnson had been the broodmare manager in their original holdings, but now he was its general farm manager and everything else. After her grandfather's death and Sam's destruction of the majority of their operation, Ben had stayed on at Richlawn Hall out of loyalty. He and Corbin had been best of friends as well as employer and employee. Her grandfather had left Ben a plot of land next to the farm for a house. Reggie hated to think what her life would be without Ben.

"Personally, it sucked," she said. Ben knew about Park. About her and Park. There was no reason to mince words.

"Did you expect anything different?"

She shrugged. "Hell, no."

"You did," he accused, "or you were hoping."

"Since when did you become a psychologist?"

"Since Corbin and I practically raised you."

She'd give him that. If it wasn't for Corbin, she'd not have had any childhood. Not with her mother dying and Sam drinking himself into oblivion more times than not. And along with Corbin came Ben. And the farm. Working on the farm, walking horses, watching the birth of foals. It was because of Corbin *and* Ben that this place was in her blood.

"What's on the agenda today?" Ben asked.

"I'm taking Park over to Culpepper's to see the yearlings. The sooner we can get him out of here, the better it will be for me."

Ben nodded agreement. "Then we can get on with it."

Reggie wanted to get on with it—with her life without the encumbrance of her father's interference and without this stupid unrequited love that was eating her up. She needed none of those complications.

Biting her lip, Reggie tried to tamp down the growing fear that something would go wrong at Culpepper's. What if Park took her best damn yearlings? He might. The man had a reputation for being a good judge of horseflesh. And he'd told her he'd done his homework. It was a simple matter to get on the Internet and find the progeny of Stuart's Legacy. When registered, the foals showed up on various public websites. Park could have already traced the bloodlines of all their yearlings. He would pick from the best they'd produced.

The prospect made her sick.

"Remember when we delivered the yearlings to Rod Culpepper's farm this year?" she asked.

Ben nodded and waited for her to continue.

"We told him we might not want to take one of our colts to the sale. We told him we were considering racing one, like Granddaddy used to do. That Granddaddy's three year limit in his will was just about up."

"Culpepper told us that would be fine," Ben said. "He said to just let him know."

"And we shook hands on it." Shaking hands used to be the way of doing business long before Reggie was born. It was the way Corbin and Rod Culpepper had always done business. No need for lawyers and pages of contracts.

"What are you thinking?" Ben asked.

"I'm thinking we need to bring home Spirit's yearling by Stuart's Legacy. Hide him in the old tobacco barn at the bottom of the hill. Keep him away from the interfering eyes of Parker Stuart."

Because a thoroughbred foal did not need to be named until February of its two-year-old year, most breeders didn't choose a name, leaving that to the final buyer. They referred to the young horse by the name of its mother, the dam, and the year of its birth.

Spiritmaker had been a great race mare. She'd set track records at Saratoga, won at a mile and a quarter, and had speed. She had the nerves of a champion and strength and power in her hindquarters. Spirit, as Reggie called her, had passed the same look onto last year's colt. Reggie's granddaddy had always said you couldn't tell how a yearling would turn out. They could certainly fool you. He said you had to go with your instinct, and Reggie's gut was telling her Spirit's yearling was a good one.

If she hid the colt from Park and kept him for herself, she could rebuild the Ward racing stable and the farm's fortunes.

"I think that's an excellent plan," Ben said nodding with agreement.

"What's an excellent plan?"

Her chest tightening, Reggie turned quickly to see Park standing outside the stall with a cheerful grin on his face. She couldn't speak. Failed to react.

"Taking you over to Culpepper's Farm before it gets too hot," Ben said, looking as innocent as a child with a hand caught in the cookie jar.

Parker hadn't been able to hear exactly what Reggie and Ben were saying. Between trying to a make a stealthy approach and their American accent with its Kentucky twang, it had been impossible for him to decipher their words completely. But he didn't think their conversation had anything to do with the heat. It had something to do with a yearling or yearlings. And Ward yearlings were fair game for him at the moment.

His doubt increased. He couldn't help it.

The older man extended a hand. "Ben Johnson. I'm farm manager."

"Nice to meet you." Parker shook the man's gnarled, work-worn hand.

"Hope you enjoy your stay." Ben nodded. He shot Reggie a look. "Best be getting at it."

After the old man left, Reggie turned from Parker and continued shoveling manure. "You're up early." Her voice was accusatory.

"I got a good night's sleep," he reported. "Although I am a bit jetlagged."

"Then maybe you'd like to put off going to Culpepper's today."

"I wouldn't miss it for the world."

Ms. Ward certainly looked different from the hillbilly wannabe of the day before. He approved of her attire today. He could even take her home to Mama in this uniform of khaki slacks and dark knit shirt. Her hair was pulled back in the same ponytail, which seemed practical given Reggie had a mane of thick hair. As hot as her workday was, she'd certainly picked a good way to wear it.

"Why don't you go back up to the house and grab yourself some breakfast?" Reggie suggested. "There are some cinnamon rolls on the island. I left the coffee on. We're bringing in the mares from the field. I can't go until that is done."

The old man had moved the tractor and manure spreader out of the center aisle and into a side building. Another worker was moving square bales of hay in a two-wheel wooden cart, separating a section of hay where it naturally divided from the bale, and dropping the flakes into stalls. But why was Reggie going with them? Why wasn't her staff taking care of the mundane chores?

Parker realized he'd only seen a handful of staff on the Ward Farm. Maybe Reggie didn't have any other workers, just the old farm manager and the few others he'd seen. That had to be it. Otherwise, why would she be doing this menial work by herself?

Bloody hell. Reggie's finances shouldn't matter to him. His objective was to further the Stuart breeding and racing venture. His father and brother depended upon him. He couldn't let this new bit of knowledge deter him.

"Hot coffee sounds good," Parker commented. "I'll meet you at the house in..." He fished for a time.

"Give me an hour," she said with a glance over her shoulder.

"An hour it is then."

Parker left the artificial light of the barn and walked into the gray, early morning sunlight. Fog lay thick over the paddocks and fields. The mares in the distance showed their pregnancies, their bellies rounded. Some had foals by their sides. Ben Johnson led two horses, both followed by long-legged foals, into the barn. When he left again, Reggie and another man were with him. Parker stood for a moment longer, watching their progress toward the nearest field. Then he turned on his heel and strode back to the house.

Two cinnamon rolls later, he was on the screened porch

cradling a mug of hot coffee in his hands and looking toward the barn and pastures. There was something peaceful about the countryside in Kentucky. Or maybe it was this place—this timeworn house on a gentle hill, overlooking pastures enclosed by four-board, black wooden fencing that undulated over the land as pretty as a picture.

Why did he suddenly feel as if he'd come home?

That was foolish. His home, his allegiance, was to his British heritage. To his family with its roots stretching back hundreds of years.

Yet, he did have an American grandmother, his mother's mother who'd taken him on vacations to Williamsburg in Virginia and Disney World in Florida. Had his drop of American blood soured him in some way? Made him think these traitorous thoughts and want something of his own...his independence?

Or was it the woman he'd seen shoveling manure in the barn? Who wasn't afraid of hard work but who seemed deathly afraid of him?

In the distance, a truck and horse trailer pulled out from the back of the barn. It turned right at the house and headed down the long, tree-lined driveway toward the motorway. In the back of Parker's mind, warning bells clamored. Did the truck have anything to do with the hush-hush conversation he'd struggled to overhear in the barn?

Parker frowned and took another sip of coffee. Was Ms. Regina Ward trying to deceive him?

CHAPTER FOUR

Culpepper's Farm looked like everything a Kentucky horse farm should be—miles of double white fence surrounding acres of bluegrass, orchard grass, alfalfa, and clover; horses in small herds, grazing with their heads down in sundrenched fields; ten, gray-metal barns with red-metal roofs and cupolas added for aesthetics. Culpepper's was a large thoroughbred operation, some of its land butted up to Ward property, and some of it, the bottom land, had actually belonged at one time to the Wards. All gone, thanks to Sam, and his string of bad luck.

This was what Ward Farm had once been. Reggie wanted to rebuild it this way again with three divisions: stallions, broodmares and yearlings.

She peered through her sunglasses at Park, who sat stoically in the passenger seat of her pickup.

"What's the matter?"

"I don't want to ruffle your feathers, but it's your driving."

She laughed. "Granddaddy always disapproved of it too. Said I drove the same way I rode horses—like a cowboy."

"Did you ever think about being a jockey?"

"Too tall." She shrugged off his suggestion. "'Sides, from the time I could walk Granddaddy had me tagging along after him, opening gates and holding horses. He groomed me for this job. I am the only heir, after all."

Reggie glanced at Park again as they came to a stop at the first barn. His mouth was pinched into a straight line. Was he thinking about his own family situation? From their short time together, she knew his position in the family aggravated him. Not the heir but the baby brother, he was relegated to doing the grunt work for the family. His father depended upon him to run the family's thoroughbred operation. His older brother counted on him to bail him out of trouble, especially after the Stuart Legacy incident when Papa Stuart had come down hard on his eldest son.

In England this summer, Park had told her he'd asked his father for part of the thoroughbred business. His father had told him younger sons didn't inherit, which had infuriated and insulted Park. Then his brother Hampton had laughed when Park asked to buy a share of the business. There'd been bad blood between the brothers after that. Too bad. Park deserved part of the operation after all the work he'd put into it, and it was time the family knew it.

As if he felt her scrutiny, Park turned toward her with a cocky grin. "I'm glad you're not jockey material. Yesterday, I enjoyed perusing your long legs in those denim hot pants."

"Okay. Enough said," she cut him off as heat flushed through her body. "Let's get this over with."

Reggie opened the door, stepped out, and slammed it shut. Without waiting for her companion, she marched toward the horse barn. As always, she admired the barn's construction and efficiency. It featured a cross aisle, in addition to the center aisle, increasing the amount of airflow running through the facility and providing extra exits for the horses. Each of its stalls had an exterior steel door with windows and a pre-hung screen between the stall and the exterior stall door that afforded ventilation and sunlight.

Rod Culpepper, the owner of the farm, met her at the main door. "Reggie."

"Thank you for meeting us." Reggie stepped into the gentleman's warm embrace. It wasn't his job to greet them. Rod had a yearling manager for that, but he was here out of respect for her grandfather. Rod gave her an extra squeeze, released her, and turned to greet Park, who had followed Reggie to the barn.

"Mr. Stuart, welcome to Kentucky."

"My pleasure." The two men shook hands.

His pleasure, all right. Reggie's heartbeat pounded and not in a good way. She'd be high-fiving everyone she encountered if she was getting four free yearlings. Park's knack for understatement was amazing.

"This is one of our yearling barns," Rod explained, leading Park into the clean, airy facility. "I've brought all of Reggie's consignments up from a lower barn to show them to you today."

She followed behind the men, envying the rubber pavers on the floor, so different from the rough asphalt in the aisle of her barn. The interior stall doors were mesh, which also helped with ventilation. The aisle was clear of all tack and equipment. In short, the place was spotless, a fine testament to Culpepper's staff.

"We consign yearlings and other horses and get them ready for various sales here in Kentucky or Saratoga." Rod described his operation as they strolled down the aisle. "We board broodmares for customer, foal them, accept layups, book our stallions to outside mares, and we even produce our own hay.

As she trailed them, Reggie searched each stall for the Spiritmaker yearling. When she didn't see him, she released a sigh of relief. Her phone call to Rod must have worked, and Juan had picked up the colt before their arrival.

"I have the Ward's fifteen yearlings ready for the sale that starts on Monday," Rod said. "We'll van the lot over to Keeneland tomorrow morning." He glanced back at Reggie. "Except, of course, for the ones you select, Mr. Stuart. I'm assuming your agent will have them picked up here."

"Yes, and we'd like to arrange for you to hold any other horses we may purchase before we ship them home."

Rod nodded. "We can handle that."

Park paused in the middle crosswalk and turned toward them. Sunshine highlighted the noble contours of his face. A warm breeze lifted a strand of black hair. He had brought a thin iPad and opened it, tapping a few times on the display screen. Then he frowned. "I thought there were sixteen yearlings for me to choose from. My notes must be wrong."

Without blinking an eye, the old horse trader replied, "I only have fifteen on the farm."

Reggie lowered her gaze and hid her smile. Thank you, Rod! Her grandfather's friend had come through! It was stupid to hang all her dreams on a yearling colt, wasn't it? But the horse was a symbol. Hadn't Granddaddy always said that without hope a person had nothing?

"Let's go outside near that big hickory tree. There's plenty of shade, and I'll have my grooms bring each horse out for your inspection."

Rod ushered them outside to three, white plastic chairs conveniently placed in the shade. They settled down, and the parade of yearlings started. The first one was a bay filly with a large star and snip on her face. The groom led her in front of them and stopped her, as she'd been schooled, while Rod ticked off her bloodlines from memory.

The second horse was an impressive chestnut colt, big for his age.

"There's power in those hindquarters," Rod remarked.

"All by Stuart's Legacy," Park stated almost as if to confirm what he already knew.

"Yes," Reggie said. "We bred all our mares to Legacy for the three years we had him."

"Did Legacy have a large book of mares?"

Rod shook his head.

"That's one thing Corbin, Reggie's granddaddy, didn't believe in. He and I were old school. We don't believe in shuttling our stallions to the Southern hemisphere. We prefer eighty to ninety mares a season, never more than one hundred."

"And you stood Stuart's Legacy at your stallion division?"

"Yes, as a favor to Corbin's granddaughter."

Reggie appreciated Rod's shrewdness. He didn't come right out and say that Stuart's Legacy was not a popular stallion in America. Maybe Park knew that. But she wasn't going to admit it. The stallion had covered several outside mares and had sustained their farm, and would continue to sustain it for two more years until all his offspring were sold. And, if she was lucky, Spiritmaker's colt might earn them money on the track.

Another filly walked in front of them. "This one is the most improved of Reggie's consignment," Rod explained. "She's put on weight. More settled in the stall. She's not big but balanced."

"Looks like a runner," Park said. He consulted his iPad, typing in a note with an index finger.

The procession continued until all fifteen yearlings had been shown.

Park rose from his chair. "I have selected a few that I want my bloodstock agent to see. Can I have him stop by later on today?"

"No problem."

"Jonathan, my agent, likes ones with a laid-back shoulder and deep pasterns. They are better suited to our European style of running. I'd like his opinion before I make my selection."

"Sounds good to me."

Somehow Reggie had been cut out of the discussion. For once, she didn't mind. What if she said something that gave away her little deception? Parker Stuart may take four of her precious babies, but he wasn't going to get the one her heart and gut said could win the Kentucky Derby.

CHAPTER FIVE

Park used the phone in the yearling office to call his British bloodstock agent, who was in Lexington for the sale. Then they climbed back into Reggie's pickup truck.

"This isn't the way to your farm," Park said when she turned left out of the Culpepper's driveway.

"I need to feed you." Heck, she wasn't about to admit there was nothing in the house for lunch.

"I'm good with that."

She glanced at him to find he was watching her with a small smile on his face. What? Didn't he ever stop staring? Was she that hideous to look at? Reggie pushed her sunglasses up on the bridge of her nose with her index finger just because it gave her something to do.

"You've produced some nice stock," Park commented.

Of course, she had. That was the goal wasn't it?

"Thanks," she said offhandedly.

"I thought you had sixteen yearlings, but we only saw fifteen."

Fear clogged Reggie's throat. Could she force out a lie? She had to. She didn't want Park to know the truth. He couldn't have the

Spiritmaker colt. "Rod told you he only has fifteen. I don't know where you got your numbers."

Stepping on the gas, Reggie took the rolling hills as if the devil pursued them. It was like riding a roller coaster over the narrow, country roads. Trees and stone fences flashed past them. She braked hard to go around a bend, tossing Park against the passenger door.

He righted himself. "I feel as if I'm taking my life in my hands riding with you."

"Sorry."

But she wasn't a bit contrite. Her ploy had worked, and the topic of the missing yearling was dropped...for now. A dead possum lay in the middle of the road. Reggie swerved to avoid it, throwing Park against her shoulder. She shrugged him off.

"Roadkill," she muttered.

"This is worse than driving in Dubai," he said with a snort of derision.

"You've been to Dubai?"

"Of course. For the Dubai World Cup."

"Of course."

Get over it. She knew he was rich. But Parker Stuart, with his fancy aristocratic British heritage, had more wealth than she could comprehend. She couldn't relate. Maybe that's one reason he scared her so badly. Maybe it wasn't just her runaway emotions or her overactive sex drive or fear of getting close to a man. She knew she was out of her league around him, and it made her feel like the hillbilly she'd played so well the previous day.

"Have you heard of Claiborne Farm?" she asked moments later.

"Who hasn't?"

"There it is, down that road to your right."

They drove past the entrance to the fabled horse farm that had stood many famous stallions—Nasrullah, Bold Ruler, Secretariat, Danzig, and several others. Then they came up quickly on the town of Paris, Kentucky. The truck bumped over the railroad tracks with the dilapidated train depot to their right.

Glancing at Park again, Reggie noticed he was taking everything in. What did he think about her part of the world? She frowned. Why should she care? Central Kentucky was the epicenter of the thoroughbred industry. She need not feel defensive.

Many of the historic buildings in the Main Street stretch of Paris had been preserved and revitalized. A few new restaurants had opened up among the antique stores and other local shops. Reggie parallel parked on the street.

"Good job," Park said.

"Thanks."

Careful to check traffic before she opened the door, Reggie stepped out of the truck. Park climbed out right on the curb. She ushered him toward the restaurant door. "I hope you're hungry. Mudd's is the best place in town to eat."

"Famished."

But, of course, this wasn't going to be fine, gourmet cuisine. Just down home Kentucky cooking made fresh daily. She hoped he'd like it. Then again, why did she care?

The owner met them at the door with a couple of menus. "Nice to see you again, Reggie."

Most everyone knew each other in a small town. "Good to see you, Hank. This is Parker Stuart, from England."

"Ah, here for the sale."

"Yes," she said. And other things.

"Sit wherever you like."

The main part of the restaurant, constructed in a restored building, was dark and cavernous with its original brick walls and high ceilings. Reggie led the way up a few steps to a bright room flanked on one side by windows. A long table of about fifteen, loud, laughing women took up much of the far end of the bright, narrow room.

White tablecloths covered the tables, but white paper was placed over each one to save on laundry bills. Would Park be appalled? Reggie didn't care. Did she?

Park pulled the metal chair out for her and helped seat her, then he took the chair opposite. Such a gentleman. Such a jerk.

Reggie opened her menu and frowned. They were too close. Sitting across from each other seemed too intimate. And she didn't need him intimate. She didn't need him anywhere but gone.

An eager, young waiter appeared by the side of the table. "What would you like to drink?"

"Sweet tea," Reggie replied.

"Make mine the same."

Reggie glanced up at him as the waiter left.

Park cocked his head to the side and said, "What? When in Rome, do as the Romans."

Her frown deepened. "I suppose."

"I figured you'd want me to get a taste of American life." His smile was amused.

"All I want you to do is go away."

Had those words really come from her mouth? Reggie was appalled.

He winked. He actually winked.

"I will, Miss Ward, and gladly once I have what I came for."

It was all she could do to keep her mouth shut. Luckily, the waiter returned with the two glasses of tea. Reggie snatched the lemon from the side of hers and squeezed it. Juice shot across the table landing on one of Park's exposed forearms, right below his rolled-up white sleeve.

His gaze never left hers as he reached over and removed the silverware rolled up in the cloth napkin. Then he dabbed the juice from his arm with the napkin.

There was something sexy in the way his stare never left her face. *Suggestive.* Suddenly, Reggie remembered licking red wine from various parts of his body. Had their "encounter" been that raw and sensual? She blushed and dropped her gaze. Damn right it had been. That was part of her fear. It would be too easy to succumb. To lose control. Not to mention, fall in love.

"Have you decided what you want to eat, miss?" the waiter asked.

"I'll take the crab cake sandwich and sweet potato fries," Reggie replied.

Park looked down at the menu then up at her. "What's good here?"

"Everything. They're known for their seafood. The burgers are good, too."

Park glanced down again then up at the waiter. "I'll have the thoroughbred burger, medium, and sweet potato fries."

"Good choices." The waiter collected the menus and left.

Why did sitting across the table from Park make her nervous? Reggie felt her face warm and her insides quiver. What could they talk about? She had no clue.

Fortunately, a young woman left the long table of chatting women and came to theirs. "Reggie? Hello! I don't want to intrude."

"Ella! What are you doing here?"

Park stood in Ella's presence, his chair scraping on the tile floor. *Damn his good manners.*

"Ella, may I introduce Parker Stuart, from England? Park, this is my friend Ella Culpepper. Her father is Rod Culpepper."

Ella's eyebrows lifted. "*That* Parker Stuart?" She turned to Park and stuck out her hand. "Glad to meet you, Mr. Stuart. I've heard a lot about you."

Park's eyes brightened as they shook hands. "I'm sure. Would you care to join us?"

"Oh, no! And please sit down." Ella turned to Reggie. "I had to drive my mother to her DAR meeting. Afterwards, they always eat at Mudd's."

"Ah, I remember," Reggie replied. Ella hated driving her mother around, but since her mother's slight stroke, chauffeuring had become part of her friend's job description. At least Ella had a mother to annoy her.

"Listen, I'm glad to have run into you. I'm having a little pool party tonight at the house. We shut down the pool tomorrow for the season. Can you two come?"

Reggie glanced at Park. She'd wondered what she was going to do with him that night. This invitation was perfect. "If Park wants to."

"My pleasure."

"Then it's decided," Ella said with a smile. "You'll be the guest of honor, Mr. Stuart."

"Call me Parker," he replied with a pointed glance at Reggie.

Ella left and their food arrived. Park dug right into his hamburger with a gusto that surprised Reggie. He must have been hungry. Her sandwich was good as usual, but she tried to be careful as she ate. She didn't want to spill the sauce down the front of her shirt and embarrass herself.

After several bites, Park sipped his tea then grimaced. "It *is* sweet," he said, but soldiered on. "What's the DAR?"

Reggie stifled a laugh. This was too funny coming from a Brit. "The Daughters of the American Revolution," she explained. "All those women at the table have ancestors who fought in the Revolutionary War."

"The American War of Independence."

"Yes, the war where we beat you damned Red Coats."

Park's slight smile spoke his amusement. "What about you? Did you have an ancestor in the war?"

"I think there was one on my grandfather's side, but he was a lowly private."

"Unlike my grandmother's ancestor, who was, I believe, a colonel in Virginia and fought under General Washington," Park said, again one-upping her.

"I guess."

Foiled again. There was no besting this man. He was too damn frustrating. Reggie took a bite of sandwich and chewed furiously so she did not need to make another comment.

Park insisted on paying for lunch, and Reggie let him. He was wealthy, after all and she was living on the bare-edge of nothing.

"May I borrow your truck," Park asked when they had pulled away from the restaurant and were heading home.

Now what?

"Do you want me to drive you some place?" she asked.

"Oh, no. I wouldn't impose. I need to go to Keeneland to meet with my agent and possibly make a few more stops before the party tonight."

"How will you know your way around?"

"If you point me toward Lexington, I can find my way," he said. "I've been to Keeneland before."

Of course, you have. Of course, you are capable of driving in a foreign country. Traffic in England had flustered Reggie. She'd been glad she didn't have to drive there.

When she didn't respond, Park added fuel to the fire. "Don't worry. I have an International Driving Permit that is honored in the United States."

Of course, he did. He had answers for everything.

"I suppose so," she answered slowly. "There's plenty of gas in the tank, and I have plenty of work to do at home."

At least she'd get rid of him for a while. Maybe she'd be able to calm her nerves with a bit of hard work. Activity is what she needed to keep her mind off things. To keep her body under control.

His first full day was almost over. Heaven help her! She had one more week to go.

CHAPTER SIX

Park arrived back at her place later than Reggie expected. She saw him come in the house carrying a shopping bag. What had he been doing? It looked as if seeing his bloodstock agent at Keeneland wasn't all that had been on his agenda.

When he came down to the truck later, Park wore new khaki cargo pants and a blue polo shirt. He'd purchased a pair of sandals too. He looked casual and relaxed and so damn sexy her heart did double-time.

What was it about Park's feet that turned her on? No, she refused to think about how many times she'd kissed each individual toe. Looking back, it seemed so totally gross. So totally unlike her.

Maybe she hadn't known herself—that wild, sexual side of herself—until she'd met Park.

No, don't go there.

The drive to the Culpepper's was strained. She felt it in her cramped stomach and in the way she gripped the steering wheel. As for Park? She thought he was silently laughing at her. *Great!* She was glad she amused him so much.

Reggie had always loved the Culpepper's home. Unlike

Reggie's house, it was quite modern, a sore thumb sticking out in the middle of horse country. But it was a family home, full of love and laughter.

Parking the truck in the circular driveway with the other cars, Reggie rested her hands on the steering wheel a moment, realizing she was in the midst of the calm before the storm. Park opened his door before she could suggest they get out and left the cab, coming around the front of the truck. Watching him, Reggie grasped the steering wheel harder. Damn! He was cute!

Like a proper British gentleman, Park opened the door for her, and she stepped out almost into his arms. He backed up giving her an inch but never took his eyes off her face. Until his gaze traveled down to her cleavage.

"Nice dress," he said, as if trying to provoke her.

She'd dressed carefully for the occasion, choosing a printed, black sleeveless dress with a V-neckline and an A-line silhouette. The knee-length, handkerchief hem showed off her long legs, and her wedge sandals added an inch to her height. He had better notice her outfit. If he hadn't, then she was slipping.

Almost at eye level now, Reggie stared at him and gave him a cool smile. She hoped her expression was saying, *you can look all you want, but you're not going to touch.* He was the most unnerving, annoying man she'd ever met.

"You look beautiful tonight."

What was it about a British accent that messed with her mind? Turned her on? Or maybe it was just *his* British accent. This handsome Brit.

Quit it! Why was she having trouble focusing tonight? Park certainly wasn't having any trouble focusing on her V-neckline and shoulders. His eyes sparkled with delight, unnerving her even more.

"Thanks." She dismissed his compliment, she hoped coolly

enough that he would think she didn't care what he thought, and tried to step around him.

He didn't move. Their bodies practically touched. Heat emanated from him, and not just body heat. Her woman's intuition sensed his desire. He lusted for her. It triggered her own desire, and she swallowed hard.

"We're late," she said.

"Are we now?"

She gazed into his eyes, drowning in the blue sea of them, and gave herself a mental shake. This was not going to happen.

Reggie lifted her chin. "Yes, we are."

As if he'd made his point, he stepped back, bowing slightly. "Then we best go in, don't you think?"

With long strides and squared shoulders, Reggie led the way around the house to the backyard. She opened a side gate and ushered Park into the pool area. Ella immediately spotted them and hurried over.

"Reggie!" Ella hugged her and whispered in her ear, "He's adorable!"

Yeah, right. Reggie didn't need adorable at the moment. She needed money. Returning Ella's hug, she merely said, "Thanks for inviting us." This was not the time or place to enlighten Ella of the nefarious nature of the guest of honor.

"Oh, I couldn't pass this up," Ella returned with a knowing look then turned to Park. "We're so glad to have you in Kentucky, Mr. Stuart."

"Call me Parker, remember? I am so happy to be here, Ms. Culpepper."

"Then you must call me Ella, Parker. Come, let me introduce you." She linked arms with him and drew him with her toward the pool.

Glad for the reprieve, Reggie took a moment to regain her composure before she slowly followed her best friend and her worst enemy poolside. She'd taken only a few steps before she realized Ella's guests consisted only of women—eleven college friends and other members of the horsey set, but all female. No wonder Mr. High-and-Mighty was the guest of honor.

Seeing Park with all those giggling, fawning women proved to be torture for Reggie. They were all over him like flies on honey. Why not? He was the only male present, and—Reggie had to admit—he was some hot male. Her girlfriends knew it, and Park soaked it all up, relishing their attention. After a while, however, it became obvious there was more to his enjoyment. Sure, Park liked the flattery, but he enjoyed watching her squirm even more. The occasional glances he sent her way told her he was playing up his role as stud to a herd of broodmares for her benefit.

Park and his companions ate from the well-laden buffet table, laughed and drank from a well-stocked bar, then laughed some more. When Reggie thought she couldn't stand any more of the party, one of the college co-eds suddenly tore off her T-shirt and shorts to reveal a skimpy bikini then dived headfirst into the pool. The other girls followed, one after the other, until only Ella, Park, and Reggie stood by the buffet table.

"I'm sorry I didn't warn you we would be swimming," Ella apologized.

"It's a pool party, isn't it?" Park replied. "I took the liberty of coming prepared, assuming there might be swimming."

"What?" Reggie couldn't believe her ears.

Or her eyes.

Slowly, with what looked to be too much pleasure, Park pulled the polo shirt over his head and slipped off his sandals. "Do you mind, ladies?"

"Oh, no!" Ella said with a giggle. "I'm glad you had so much foresight."

How many times during those three weeks in London had Reggie witnessed Park rip off his shirt that way? Too many to count. She refused to think about it.

With his gaze locked on hers, Park unzipped his cargo pants and stepped out of them. Slowly. One leg at a time.

What was he doing stripping in front of them? Her friends were hanging on the side of the swimming pool, whistling and catcalling. He was making a spectacle of himself. What a jerk.

Underneath the khaki pants, Park wore a pair of Nike swim shorts. They were Spandex or something. Bright blue with a black band. And they hugged his butt and waist, showing off the bulging promise Reggie definitely wanted to forget.

She felt her face flame.

"I'm sorry you didn't come prepared," he said.

"I'll bet you are," Reggie scoffed.

He winked and turned toward the pool. "Coming, ladies!"

Going to the deep end, Park dived expertly into the water. His head bobbed to the surface, and he tossed water from his hair with a headshake. Then the girls surrounded him. His deep laughter joined with their shrill giggling and splashing. All Reggie could do was gape.

"Come on." Ella gave her hand a tug. "You're coming to my bedroom. I'm loaning you a swimsuit."

Reggie followed Ella through the house to her bedroom.

"You've got to be kidding?" she said when her friend laid a bright aqua bikini on the bed.

"Not in the least."

"That's not a swimsuit. It's a scrap of cloth."

"True, but a very expensive and stylish scrap of cloth," Ella replied.

The skimpy, underwire halter tied together at the neck and

back. The tiny bottom clung to Reggie's hips, exposing her flat waist and long legs. If Park had disapproved of her cutoffs and tank top, what would he think of this attire?

"I might as well be naked," Reggie complained when she looked in the mirror.

"Maybe. But you're not."

"I can't do this."

"Why not? There's not an ounce of fat on you. You look like a damn model, for heaven's sakes."

Reggie turned left and right in front of Ella's full mirror. She did look good. But she was uncomfortable wearing the bikini. Work, the farm, and the horses all came first. Thinking about herself and what she wanted rarely crossed her mind.

"Besides," Ella remarked, "he's already seen you naked. This will remind him."

Shocked, Reggie spun and faced her friend. "How do you know that?"

Ella shook her head. "It doesn't take a mind reader to know what goes on between two people who are *together* for three weeks."

Reggie had told Ella that much. She hadn't expected her friend to be so good at reading between the lines.

"And by the look of him, Parker's just egging you on with our friends. He's just trying to make you jealous."

"Jealous?"

"If you ask me, he's not over you, Reggie."

"You're wrong. The only reason he's here is because of the yearlings."

"I doubt that," Ella retorted. "The man's hot for you. Now, go out there and make him squirm."

Was she jealous of the attention the other girls gave Park? Well, sure she was. She might deny it to Ella, but she couldn't lie to herself. She might not be over Park, but that didn't mean he was good for her. Or that he wanted anything more than his cut of her bloodstock. No, if he'd really cared about her, he would have replied to her text. Or sent her an email. Or called. June was a lifetime away. Parker wasn't serious about her.

But she could seriously try to get under his skin.

When she and Ella, who had donned her own bikini, emerged from the house, Reggie walked barefoot to the edge of the pool. She waited until Park looked over then dropped the towel she'd wrapped around her torso. It puddled at her feet. Park stopped playing and watched as Reggie stretched out a toe and tested the water. Satisfied, she sat on the edge of the pool, cupped a bit of water in her hands and dribbled it down her leg.

He swam over to her. "You'll never get used to the temperature that way."

"I'll manage." She ignored him, turning up her nose.

"Rubbish."

That's when he splashed her. The cold water cut right into her skin, it seemed.

"Hey!" she yelped.

"The only way to get used to it is to endure the shock to the system. Do it quickly then it's over. Come on, Reggie, chin up. You can take it."

"I don't need direction from you, Parker Stuart."

"Ah, you used my real name. Sounds brilliant coming from your lips."

Reggie kicked her foot in the water splattering Park's face. He wiped his eyes quickly with his fingertips.

"So that's the way it's going to be," he said. He grabbed Reggie's wrist and pulled her face first into the pool. She came up struggling and spluttering, but Park was there to steady her.

"Not fair! Get off me!"

"It's the only way to accustom yourself."

"Bull."

She was too aware of his hands on her waist, caressing her skin with his fingers. The water buoyed her. It lapped around them protecting them in a wet cocoon. The girls' laughter faded into background noise. Only the two of them mattered—alone together in a swirl of sensuality. She wanted to struggle, to pull herself away, but his gaze held her as captive as his hands on her body.

His arrogant grin disappeared.

"You are a beautiful woman," he whispered. "If we were alone, I'd untie this silly bow at the back of your neck."

For a split second, Reggie longed for him to kiss her. She fought to stifle her own desire. They were opponents. She couldn't let herself forget.

"And you, sir, are a bully and a thief," she told him.

"Ah, it all comes back to the horses."

Reggie tried to pull away. "Doesn't everything?"

"Not for me."

"Then you have it over me, my lord thief." She focused her gaze over his shoulder to the other women in the pool, looking anywhere but at Park.

He pulled her hips toward him. Now, he had her full attention. Even with the water swirling around them, she felt the heat of his erection through the scraps of their swimsuits.

"I am no thief, and you are no innocent," he said between clenched teeth. "Your father and my brother set this game into motion. But neither is man enough to see it through."

"And I suppose you are?"

"I'm man enough for this job," he said, his grip tightening on her waist. "And in June, I proved I was man enough for you."

CHAPTER SEVEN

Why hadn't he kept his hands to himself? The swimming party had been a game changer, and putting his hands on Reggie's body had been a big time blunder. He'd been close enough to kiss her. A deep fear rumbled in Parker's gut. Would he be able to love her and leave her when the time came?

After a sleepless night berating himself, Sunday morning arrived much too early for Parker. When he made it downstairs to the kitchen, the room was dark and silent. He flipped on the overhead lights. Hot coffee in the coffeepot and a plate of blueberry muffins told him that Reggie had come and gone.

Good. He needed the respite. Last night had been hard on him. Seeing her in a bikini reminded him too much of Reggie in his flat, slipping naked from the shower and into his bed. Besides, the cat and mouse game with all those hysterical women had been bloody painful, not as much fun as he'd let on.

He fixed his coffee and grabbed a muffin, taking them both outside to the porch. Ceiling fans flapped slowly, hardly breaking the stickiness that seeped into his skin. How did a person live with such humidity? Some sort of insect whirred in the grass, its high-pitched buzz annoying. A thick gray haze glazed the sky.

God, these farmers need rain. The late summer drought had turned the grass dry and brittle. It couldn't be good for raising horses.

It wasn't good for his spirits either. He felt hot and grumpy—awash in emotions he thought he'd put aside.

Parker finished the muffin then slowly sipped his coffee. The empty pastures were a symbol of the Ward family's fall from the heights of thoroughbred dominance. He knew the mares were inside because of the heat, but Reggie had been forced to ship her yearlings to a consigner, because she didn't have land or staff enough to finish the job herself. It was a shame.

From what he'd seen, she had raised good horses. Stuart's Legacy had been a fine, productive stallion in England. He'd carried on his supremacy in the States. But his bloodline had been only half the combination. Reggie's mares had produced excellent stock. He'd tell her so when he took his four horses from her.

Parker's heart protested, but what else could he do? It was the deal. It was his responsibility. The Stuart racing team depended upon him. His father counted on him. And so did his brother, Hampton, the good-for-nothing bastard who'd eventually inherit the whole damn thing.

The way things had to be didn't sit right with Parker. As loyal as he was to his father and his family name, he often regretted his position. The luck of his birth meant Hampton got it all. His older brother could party and throw away the inheritance Parker struggled to protect. Their father loved the horses. They meant everything to him, and he trusted Parker to keep things running smoothly. To right Hampton's mistakes and fix his screw-ups.

The night his brother revealed he'd gambled away Stuart's Legacy had been rough on everyone. His father had yelled and cursed. His mother had cried and tried to protect her favorite son. Hampton had begged forgiveness and promised to make it right. But Parker had been the one who'd put his nose to the grindstone and dealt with the loss of the stallion. By booking other up-and-coming stallions to Stuart mares, he'd produced several nice crops of yearlings without the fabled Stuart stallion.

In the end, though, Hampton had made it right with his father by winning against Sam Ward in June. The four yearlings, culled from the Ward herd, would make things better between Hampton and his father. Another triumph for his older brother. But Parker had been sent to do the dirty work.

So be it.

Then why had doing his duty become so onerous? Why did he consider himself the fall guy?

Reggie rested her arms on the top fence railing near the old tobacco barn. Sunshine broke through the early morning haze. It would be a blistering day. She gazed across the pasture at the Spiritmaker colt. He'd been separated from the mares in a far field, but shared a paddock with the farm's teaser stallion, a Shetland pony named Mr. Too Little that they used to determine how receptive a mare would be to the thoroughbred stallion.

She yawned. Maybe when Park left the country, she'd finally get some sleep. Last night's pool party had been a killer. Not to mention the endless tossing and turning once she'd climbed into bed.

Gosh, she'd longed for him to kiss her. The desire had been overpowering. Seeing him in swim trunks brought back so many vivid memories. So many emotions.

Reggie knew yearning for something that would never happen was pointless. She had to buck up her resolve. Not back down.

Bottom line, Park and his family were out to destroy hers. It was her father's fault, of course. Everything was his fault in one way or another—from being such a drunk, from not being there when her mother died, to gambling away her heritage. She couldn't let her father win in the end by allowing the Ward family farm to go under.

She couldn't let Park win either. That would signify how far the Wards had fallen.

Reggie set her jaw with a renewed determination. Only when she was with her horses did she know what was truly important. Not her silly emotions or overactive libido.

Ben stood beside her at the fence. "Jimmy's a good looker. That 'un might just be our ticket to the Kentucky Derby."

At Culpepper's, the chestnut colt they'd hidden from Park yesterday had acquired the nickname of "Jimmy." It was easier than always referring to him by the name of his dam and year of birth, which was how it usually happened until the Jockey Club granted approval for a registered name.

Yearlings grew in spurts. Sometimes the hind end grew then the withers caught up to the back. Jimmy was balanced all over. He had the *look*. Only time would tell if he had the heart of a champion too.

As part of the Culpepper's consignment prep, Jimmy had learned to walk in an automated horse walker, trotting sometimes, while wearing a girth, reins and a bit. He'd been taught to love being handled, especially the cool-down after exercising—a strong spray of water with a groom scraping off the sweat. Most yearlings went out at seven in the evening to keep their coats from bleaching out in the summer sun. After all, the purpose was to get them ready for the big Keeneland September Yearling Sale. They had to look good, because whatever the buyer saw, the buyer believed. However, many a good-looking prospect never made it on the track. Often the cheaper horses that weren't as good to look at made the best racehorses. Seattle Slew, for instance. A seller and a buyer just never knew for sure.

"He's a bit lonely," Ben commented. "He's used to being with his herd mates. Too Little isn't a good companion. The pony thinks this paddock belongs to him."

"Well, let's bring Jimmy in and give him a good brushing."

Ben brought the colt from the paddock into the converted tobacco barn. Once a booming Kentucky industry, tobacco barns had been built to house the leaves as they dried and cured. Now, hulking shells of unused barns dotted the landscape. Fortunately, her granddaddy had renovated this one. With its tall roof, plank walls, and overall design, the barn offered great ventilation, which was critical for keeping horses.

Reggie tied the young horse in a stall with a measure of feed in his bucket. As Jimmy munched his breakfast, she slowly used the currycomb on his reddish coat—around and around to loosen the mud from the skin. Next, she applied the hard-bristled brush to remove the dirt and hair. Reggie took her time. She certainly had no desire to face Park just yet. Besides, grooming was always therapeutic for her, as well as for the horse.

This youngster was going to be her "big horse," her ticket to success. She loved the feel of his muscles beneath his gleaming red coat. She loved visualizing him racing down the stretch, the famed Twin Spires in the background.

As she worked, Reggie's daydreaming took a turn, away from the horse and the farm to the big attraction between her and Park. When they were together, it simmered between them as if it were a living thing. She couldn't speculate on its cause other than being certain sex was a large part of it. She fought temptation whenever she saw him. Whenever he touched her. Better for her to stay completely away.

But *what if* this grand passion between her and Park could somehow work out? Could they find a way to bridge the gap of their upbringing? Their expectations? Would Park give up his highfalutin' family to make a life with her in America?

Who was she kidding? There was too much was at stake...for both of them.

Heck, a girl could dream couldn't she? It was an enchanting dream. But a pipe dream.

She'd never bring up the subject with him. Oh, no, she didn't have that much courage. It was easier to fight through her emotions. Hide her fears. As the daughter of an alcoholic, she'd been vulnerable most of her life. Just as she'd been vulnerable last night to Park's charms and his sexy, hunky body. And she didn't like the feeling.

She didn't like it one damn bit.

The sun was bearing down hot on her head when she hiked up the gentle knoll from the creek bottom toward the main house. She was sweaty and hungry but had no clue what there was to eat in the refrigerator. Entering the back porch, Reggie was pleased not to find Park in the kitchen or the back stairway leading up to the second floor. She showered quickly, donned a clean pair of khakis and a dark green shirt, grabbed her purse, and headed to her pickup.

Driving down the long, shaded driveway to the main road, she spotted Park walking up it, a canvas bag à la Indiana Jones slung over his shoulder. What had he been up to?

She pulled alongside and pushed the button to lower her window.

"Hello, beautiful," he said without so much as a proper good morning.

"Good morning, to you too," she fired back. On the tip of her tongue was the question, *what are you doing?* but she didn't ask.

He had no such hesitation. "Where are you heading on this bright, sun-shiny day?"

"Are you kidding? It is as hot as Hades out here."

He shrugged as if the heat didn't bother him, but she could see a trickle of sweat glistening on the side of his face. He wasn't as oblivious to the temperature as he liked to pretend.

"I must be getting used to the climate," he said in his snooty British accent. "I'm certainly beginning to enjoy the heat." He raised an eyebrow and stared pointedly at her.

Of course, he meant to flummox her. And he did. Her heart beat rapidly. She gripped the steering wheel, thankful sunglasses prevented him from reading her eyes.

"I hope you don't succumb to a heat stroke," Reggie replied with a sharp edge to her voice. "It's pretty far to a hospital."

"I'm sure I'll manage to avoid it."

"I'm sure you will. Something tells me you manage quite well at whatever you do."

She pushed the button to shut the automatic window. It whirred up, blocking the glare from Park's gaze. Putting the truck into drive, Reggie pulled away. She was barreling down the highway before she realized she hadn't told him she was going to the grocery store.

But he hadn't told her what he'd been doing either.

After putting groceries away and sticking chunks of stew meat, carrots, and potatoes into a crockpot and adding a packet of seasoning and water, Reggie was ready to hunt for Park. But she had no clue where to start. A quick glance at the mares and their long-legged foals in the barn proved to her he wasn't there. She walked back to the house. Not on the porch either. And she sure as heck wasn't going up to his bedroom to search for him.

When she pushed open the door from the kitchen to the dining room, she found him sitting quietly at the table. His back was to the door, and he was facing the light of the window. What the hell was he up to? Heavy paper was spread out in front of him. A flat box of colored pencils was to his left.

She stole up behind him. He didn't hear her. "What are you doing?" she asked.

He flinched, startled, and turned to glare at her. "What the bloody hell? Why are you creeping up on a chap? Have you no respect?"

"I didn't know where you were."

"Not much danger of me leaving the premises. You took the only vehicle."

She had to give him that. He turned away from her, back to whatever he was doing. She approached slowly, noticing his black shag of hair and broad shoulders.

No, don't go there.

In front of him on the table was a lightly penciled drawing of Richlawn Hall atop its knoll. It was flanked on one side by the long, tree-lined driveway and on the other by rolling green pasture.

"It's beautiful," she said in an impressed tone. "I didn't know you painted."

"When you were at my flat, you admired my watercolors of the North Devon coast."

Had she? Reggie seemed to not remember much about that time except the contours of this man's body. But thinking back, she recalled framed pictures of a rugged coastline and golden sandy beaches. She'd thought them lovely. She remembered telling him so.

"But you never told me you painted them."

Park glanced up and grinned wickedly. "I had other things on my mind."

Of course, he did. And she did too. Reggie didn't enjoy dragging up those memories. "May I sit down and watch?"

He inclined his head. "If you're quiet. I need to concentrate."

Reggie pulled out a chair and sat, propping her elbows on the table and resting her chin in her fists. He used what appeared to be normal colored pencils, filling in his rough outlines, shading, adding different colors. His strokes were quick and sure. He knew what he was doing, and he was good at it. The painting took shape when he started to put water over his colors. Dipping a small soft paintbrush into a shot glass of water, he washed out the color, deftly as if he'd had plenty of practice.

"It looks like watercolors," she said breathlessly.

"It is, luv. These are water-soluble pencils. Much easier to carry with me when I travel."

For the first time, he slipped and called her "luv" like he'd done in London.

The painting of her home blossomed before her eyes. But Reggie was totally in awe of Park. She could watch him forever—watch those strong hands with gentle strokes skimming across the white paper, his teeth gnawing slightly on his lower lip as he focused totally on his work, the furrow of his black brow.

Her appraisal must have gotten to him. He glanced up. "What?"

"Nothing."

"You're staring at me," he accused.

"You surprise me, that's all."

"I like to keep people guessing."

"Well, I never guessed you had such talent."

He shrugged. "Doesn't put food on the table."

"Then why do you do it?"

"It relaxes me," he said, "and I've needed a lot of relaxing on this trip."

Reggie squirmed in her seat and decided to ignore his remark. "I wish I had talent like that."

He made a dismissive gesture. "It's nothing." Then after a few more strokes, he looked up and surveyed her face. "Raising good horses is a fine art. You're like your grandfather, Reggie. You have the talent. A good artist lets her work speak for itself. Those yearlings over at Culpepper's speak to your gift."

Her breathing seemed to stop, and her mouth dropped open slightly. That was the nicest thing he'd ever said to her—that *anyone* had ever said to her.

"I mean it, luv," he said.

He put down his brush, reached across the table, lifted her jaw to shut her mouth, then leaned over and kissed her.

CHAPTER EIGHT

She let his lips linger. Wanted them to linger. Leaning in, Reggie kissed him back. Deepening their contact, her mouth opened under his. This was how it was meant to be. Needed to be. Had to be.

But dammit, this was Park! Her enemy!

Reggie jerked her head back and scowled at him. She swiped a hand over her lips, wiping away the kiss. "What are you doing?"

He grinned, a self-satisfied grin. "What do you think I'm doing? I'm letting you remember how it was."

She jumped up, shoving her chair back. "I don't want to remember. You've come here to ruin my life."

"And you left me in London with a text message. A text message, Reggie."

His accusation was damning. She'd done that. Sure. But she'd needed to. She couldn't lose control. She'd had to break the spell he'd had over her. It hadn't been safe. Falling in love wasn't safe, especially so quickly. Especially when it wasn't love but just good sex.

He rose and faced her. "How do you think I felt?"

His soft words poured out a hurt she hadn't expected. But she couldn't do anything about it. Or about him and whatever they had those crazy three weeks in London. At the end of the week, Parker Stuart would return to London with four of her prized yearlings. By God, she couldn't let herself forget that. It was the reason he'd come to Kentucky. The only reason.

She pulled herself erect, jutting out her chin. It didn't matter if her insides were topsy-turvy. It didn't matter that she felt like a jerk. All that mattered was her farm. The Ward legacy.

"I've put a stew in the crockpot," Reggie said, her voice hardly a whisper. "Give it a couple of hours, and it should be ready to eat."

"Where are you going?"

"I've got to take care of the horses."

"The horses. Always the horses."

"Yes, dammit! They are always there. They depend upon me. They're my life."

She turned to flee, but he caught her upper arm. Her flesh burned where he touched her.

"You're running away again."

The charge stung. She couldn't deny it any more than she could do anything about it. She'd run all her life, ever since her mother died and she'd run from the house in tears. Granddaddy had found her in the barn, hugging the orange tabby barn cat. Somehow, the shuffling of the horses in their stalls had soothed her. Grounded her. Made her feel okay.

Reggie shook her arm free. "I've got to check on the horses. They need me."

Glancing for a second into his eyes, she saw a strange look of anger and pain. She couldn't make sense of it. Didn't want to. Not now. Not ever.

Why in the bloody hell had he kissed her?

Parker glanced sideways at a very subdued Reggie. Behind the wheel of her pickup, she was tightlipped and pale. But beautiful. Always beautiful. She wore the same dress from the pool party, the one that had turned him on so much. And she had plastered those damn sunglasses on her face, concealing her eyes—and her thoughts—from him.

It was damn awkward, sitting there beside her in the cramped truck cab. She smelled delicious, a mixture of outdoors and lavender. The vibrant energy she exuded transferred itself to him. Made him jittery. Made him angry.

Reggie had made it perfectly clear last night. Horses before him. What did he expect? He'd played the fool's game by hoping for more. She'd left him, hadn't she? And there was no regret on her part. To her, he was a nemesis. The bad guy out to ruin her life.

But what did he want? Love her and leave her? That had been his goal. Take the horses, as was his due. Take what he could from her and return to London. Return to life, as he knew it, life that was sane and secure.

Was it sane? Was he happy there in England?

He'd been happy until Reggie had come into his life in June. Now he didn't like himself very much. Didn't like the queasy feelings swirling in his gut. The confusion in his brain.

She'd stayed away from him last night. Alone, he'd eaten the beef stew, which had turned out very good to his surprise. He'd downed a bottle of Bud Light with the meal, wishing he'd had a bottle of Guinness instead. Reggie hadn't shown up for breakfast either. The coffeepot had been on as usual, and he drank a cup. However, he couldn't force down another blueberry muffin. In fact, he hadn't been able to eat a thing.

Today was the big day—the start of the Keeneland September Yearling Sale. Buyers from across the United States as well as many foreign countries participated in the auction. The sale lasted almost two weeks. Approximately four thousand horses were cataloged. Some not reaching their reserve would be withdrawn by their breeders, others sold for enormous prices. And some, like the four he was taking from Culpepper's farm, would never make it to the sales ring.

Parker had been to the sale many times in the last ten years. First, he'd come with his father then alone, meeting his bloodstock agent who helped him with selecting and shipping the horses back to England. This time was different. With four free horses already under his belt, he was only in the market for a couple more. He hoped to purchase them today or tomorrow so he could keep his Friday departure schedule.

Too much time in Kentucky wouldn't be good for him. Not this year.

West of Lexington, with the Blue Grass Airport on the other side of the motorway, they entered the Keeneland Association grounds. As they drove past the large, green, cast-iron KA posts, Parker was transported back in time to a world of sprawling, manicured grounds and beautiful, serene shade trees. This was the heart of the horse business—one thousand acres of dedication and professionalism.

After Reggie parked the truck, they walked silently into the Sales Pavilion. Japanese, Arab, and European buyers mingled with the cream of the American racing world, such as famed trainers Steve Asmussen and Bob Baffert. Parker paused at the glass windows, separating the sales arena floor from the rest of the pavilion. The six-hundred-and-fifty seats were mostly empty. Most buyers were back in the barns, examining their prospects until closer to the noon starting time.

Everything in the pavilion spoke of money and tradition—the paneled walls, displays of expensive artwork, and the deference given to those in attendance. No one knew who might be the next big spender—an Arab sheik, rugged cowboy, or British aristocrat.

The folks at Keeneland treated all the patrons like they had a million dollars in their hip pockets.

Reggie had left Parker, but returned with two bound paperback catalogs.

"Here," she said, handing one to him.

It was the first time she'd said anything to him all day.

"Thanks."

She still wore her sunglasses, even indoors. The tinted lenses blocked his view. But maybe it didn't matter. He knew what she was thinking, and he had a job to do.

"Let's check out some of the other consignees."

He imagined her gaze was piercing. "I take it you've already selected the ones you want from my farm."

He nodded. "Yes. I gave Rod my list yesterday. My bloodstock agent helped me select them, and he's already arranged for transportation home."

Her lips thinned. Her jaw tensed. "Fine. That's done then."

"Yes, it's done."

Reggie turned and walked around the perimeter of the arena. Parker caught up to walk by her side. They came out into the holding area. Big doors were open to the outdoor area where the horses walked before their hip numbers were called. Reggie led the way through glass doors to a brick patio and up a set of steps. The back of Keeneland's grandstands faced them. However, instead of going into the racetrack, they headed along the road to the barns.

The area was packed with buyers and buzzed with festive chatter and the occasional high-pitched neigh of a horse. Each barn tried to outdo the other, hoping happy customers would be enticed into spending money. Barn colors differentiated the otherwise cookie-cutter buildings. Potted plants decorated the welcome desks, hung from the rooftops and over the railings separating the customers from the stalls. A huge sign plastered each stall door, listing the hip number of the horse occupying the stall, its sex—colt or filly—and the names of the sire and the dam.

Parker's mood couldn't help but lighten. He loved this—dozens of horses going in and out of stalls with their showmen to parade before dozens of buyers, hooves crunching on crushed stone, horses sometimes kicking or rearing. He loved the activity and the sense of urgency. He loved the expensive horseflesh, the best in the world.

Pausing, he flipped through the catalog. Each colt or filly was described in it, identified by hip number, with a foaling date and lengthy pedigree going back several generations. "I want to see a colt in Barn Three," he said. "It's right this way."

Reggie tossed her ponytail. "I know where Barn Three is located."

"Of course, you do," he said then muttered to himself, "of course, you do."

Hip number thirty-nine was a colt by Tiznow by a very good mare. An attendant for the consigner brought the colt out of its stall and posed the horse in front of Parker. The bay's flanks had sweat on them. It was a hot day, and this was the yearling's first time away from the farm. Parker circled him, nodding.

"Walk him for me, if you please."

The attendant led the colt around the walkway, letting him stride out along a pathway. They circled an oak tree and returned to Parker.

"Thank you," Parker said to the attendant who led the horse away.

Reggie didn't say a word, merely standing off to the side, watching. Occasionally, her jaw moved as if she gritted her teeth or she'd shift her stance as if annoyed. How she balanced on those awful platform sandals, he didn't know.

More for his own benefit to assess his judgment, he commented, "The colt is clean of limb. Nothing is offset about him."

To his surprise, Reggie nodded. "He should be suited for European racing."

"Yes," he said. "I was thinking just that. I've looked at his X-rays and had him scoped. I simply wanted one more look at him."

They surveyed each other, standing in the blistering sun, until Reggie raised her chin. "Do you want to see any others?"

"Yes." Parker consulted his catalog. "Let's go up to Barn Twenty-five. Then we need to head to the Pavilion."

Reggie found the two seats in the arena marked with the Ward Farm name. The sale had started minutes earlier, but the director-style folding seats were mostly empty.

A tall, impressive auctioneers' desk formed the backdrop of the sales ring in the center of the floor. An electronic board displayed each horse's hip number and the current bid or final sales price once the bidding ended. Led by the consigner's attendant, each yearling entered from the back of the ring behind the auctioneers' desk, was transferred to a Keeneland handler in a green blazer, then stood as its fate was decided. When the "sold" sign flashed, the handler gave the yearling back to the original attendant. As the next yearling entered, the sold horse left by the opposite door, where it would be vanned away to its new life.

Other Keeneland associates in dark green blazers and striped ties prowled the arena floor, spotting bidders and transferring that information back to the auctioneer. Reggie's blood raced with the thrill of the auction. She couldn't help it, no matter the circumstances, because raising and loving good horses was her whole life, her heritage from her granddaddy. This first day, Ward Farm didn't have any horses going to auction. Keeneland scheduled only the most prized yearlings, the ones with the best pedigrees, in the first few days of the sale. That was okay. With any luck at all, Reggie would sell her remaining eleven horses and have enough money for operating expenses for another year.

"Glad to see you've removed your sunglasses," Park whispered as he slipped into the chair next to her.

"Shhh!" Reggie hushed. Too much movement or noise and a person might accidently buy a horse.

He settled in his seat and opened his catalog. Today, Park wore hip-clinging blue jeans and his Armani suit coat. He looked casual and relaxed but blue-blooded, a man with money. Reggie noticed he caught the eye of a man, who walked down an aisle on the other side of the room. They exchanged looks, then the other man took a seat.

"Are you going to buy anything?" she asked.

"Shhh!" Park smirked.

So it would be tit-for-tat with him. She'd shushed him, and now, he did it to her. Then he leaned against her shoulder and said softly in her ear, "Wait and see."

The feel of the fabric of his suit coat against her bare arm comforted her in some odd, inexplicable way. She would miss him when he left on Friday—just as she had missed him when she'd left London in June. Tamping down the thought, she turned her attention to the auction.

The sale went like clockwork. An assembly line of expensive, well-bred horseflesh was presented, one fine animal after another. Hip number thirty-nine entered the sales ring before she knew it. Reggie excitedly jabbed Park's arm with her elbow. He covered her bare arm with a warm hand to quiet her.

The bidding began, fast and furious, going up in twenty-five thousand dollar increments. The auctioneer's singsong voice added to the urgency and excitement. Someone in the far side of the room responded to every raised figure or subtle nod of a head. A burly man and one dressed in Arab robes countered. A bidding war commenced. Back and forth, back and forth, until only the burly man and a person on the far side of the room were left battling it out.

When the gavel came down and the green "sold" showed on the board, the horse had been purchased for five hundred and seventy-five thousand dollars.

"That's more than half a million dollars," Reggie said in awe.

"I know," Park replied, matter-of-factly. "I just bought myself a horse."

CHAPTER NINE

Reggie had known Parker was rich, but seeing him spend half a million dollars on a yearling drove it home as nothing else before had. She wasn't envious but, oh, to have that kind of money just once in her life. What she could do with it made her mouth water.

"Let's get something to eat," Park whispered. "I'm famished."

Reggie held her head high as she followed Park up the steps and out of the arena. She might not be able to compete with Parker's wealth or prestige, but her Kentucky heritage was a proud one. In that respect, she had nothing of which to be ashamed.

"I guess your credit is good," she remarked once they'd reached the outer pavilion.

"The best."

"Yes, of course."

Of course. Mr. High-and-Mighty had everything taken care of. Everything under control.

He took her elbow and ushered her down the hall into one of the dining rooms set around it. They found seats at an empty table. A green-coated waiter took their drink order then invited them to serve themselves at the buffet. Park must have been hungry as he piled his plate high. Reggie suspected she hadn't fed him well enough during his stay, but that wasn't her problem. She'd never claimed to be a cook and housekeeper. If he wanted to be coddled, he'd have to find another woman.

What was the matter with her? Why did she think like that? Why did she think of herself as his "woman"? As if three weeks gave her some sort of dibs on him? She had to stop this crazy self-talk. And stop it fast.

"You're not hungry?"

Reggie surveyed her plate. She'd filled it mostly with salad and a little fried catfish. She shook her head. "Not particularly."

"You'll never have enough energy to do all the work you do without eating more."

"I don't see that it's any of your concern." Her reply had been snippy when he'd only been making conversation, but she didn't care.

He glanced up at her, fork poised over his plate. "Probably not."

Reggie had the feeling he wanted to say something more but had thought better of it. Instead, he dug once more into his food. She toyed with her own meal.

"About last night," Park said a few minutes later. "I got carried away. I'm sorry."

He wasn't looking at her. His focus was on his plate with its diminishing quantity of food. What was he driving at?

"Are you speaking about the kiss or your comment about my horse-breeding abilities?"

A small smile tugged at the side of his lips, but he kept his head down. "Your talent with horses is not in question. I'm speaking about my forwardness. I shouldn't have kissed you."

She straightened her shoulders. "No. You shouldn't."

He looked up then. "But I received the impression you didn't mind initially."

"Your impression was wrong."

He cocked his head. "So I discovered."

He took another bite of his Kentucky hot brown, an open-faced sandwich of turkey and bacon, covered in Mornay sauce, and chewed it slowly. Finally, he said, "You're very good at the silent treatment. Most women are."

She lifted her chin. Her appetite was totally gone. "I'm not most women."

He grinned a little. "Aren't you?"

Reggie fought the burst of anger and bit her tongue. No, she wasn't like other women. She was different. She put her family and farm first over a half-baked relationship with a man she didn't really know.

Relationship? Hell, it had been purely sex. Nothing more.

"I don't see how you are much different from most men, simply thinking with the lower part of your anatomy. You want nothing more than that."

Park put down his fork and clutched his chest over his heart. "Ah, you've found me out!"

"Stop making fun of me."

"You wound my heart, Reggie. I'm not making fun."

"Yes, you are, but you don't have a leg to stand on. You and I are not so very different, Parker Stuart."

"Ah, my given name!"

Annoyance rolled through her, and she wanted to throttle him. "You put horses and family ahead of anything else. Just like I do. It has to be that way to survive in this business. You're in Kentucky now to take my horses and buy others. Nothing else."

"Yes, thank you for reminding me."

She reached for her cold, sweating glass, more for something to do with her hands than for anything else. She picked it up and took a drink of sweet tea, scowling at him over the rim.

"Parker?"

Thankfully, a young man with an Irish accent interrupted them.

Park looked up then turned to Reggie. "Reggie, this is my agent, Jonathan Reynolds. Jonathan, Miss Regina Ward."

The rugged-looking man nodded at her. "Miss."

Reggie nodded in return, acknowledging him.

Parker gestured to an empty chair at their table. "Why don't you sit down and join us, Jonathan?"

The man took the empty seat next to Reggie, took a yeast roll from the basket on the table, and broke it in two.

"How did it go?" Parker asked.

"Smoothly. I've arranged for Culpepper to take the new colt to his farm. He'll keep all of them until Friday."

All of them. The agent was talking about *her* yearlings. Her babies. Reggie gritted her teeth. At least Park didn't know about Jimmy. Her little secret. For once, she was getting the best of him. And he didn't even know it.

She started to rise. "You gentlemen are talking business. If you'll excuse me?"

Park laid a hand over her wrist. "Don't leave. After we eat, we'll walk up to Culpepper's barn and look at the consignees."

Reggie didn't want to remain there and listen to these men talk about taking her horses. A tumultuous ache rumbled in her stomach. She swallowed hard but forced herself to sit back down.

Only later, did she realize it was the first time she hadn't run away from an unpleasant situation.

Parker was glad Jonathan had secured the Tiznow colt. The yearling had promise, and his father would be happy. Yet, Parker wasn't so happy about what this whole arrangement was doing to Reggie. It couldn't be prevented, of course. He had a responsibility to take her yearlings. He just wasn't sure if he could act on his plan to seduce her. Doing so proved to be tougher than he'd thought.

With the pressure off because he'd gotten the big colt, Parker was all too pleased to let Jonathan handle the other bids for the week. They'd planned on buying at least one more yearling that day, and if they didn't have luck with a winning offer, there was always tomorrow and more horses.

After their lunch, Parker escorted Reggie to Culpepper's barn.

"Ben is working today," she told him. "Rod needs the help, and it's good money."

"Something tells me you'd be working too, if I wasn't here."

Reggie paused and glanced up at him. "Something tells me you're right."

He made no comment. He didn't need to. Her words spoke volumes about the state of affairs at Ward Farm.

The same process was going on in Culpepper's stabling area as they'd witnessed earlier in Barn Three. Buyers requested to see a horse by hip number and grooms brought the yearling out for inspection. It was hot, exhausting work for the grooms, because each horse had to be spit-polished and ready for review at any time before the sale.

Parker didn't have any particular yearling to look at. He'd done his homework and seen much of the early book offerings on Saturday afternoon, when he'd paid a visit to his agent. Besides, he suspected Reggie wanted to talk to the consigner alone to find out which of her horses weren't going to the sale but were going to England with him instead.

"You go ahead," he said. "I think I'll get a glass of tea and sit in the shade until you're ready."

She glanced his way, but he was unable to read her expression because of those damn sunglasses. She didn't say anything, only nodded and left, her long strides eating up the ground to where Rod Culpepper stood with a couple of well-to-do buyers.

After taking a plastic cup of cold, sweet tea brimming with ice from the refreshment table, Parker settled down on a green park bench in front of the stable area. He was content to watch the activity around him. He wanted to remember this day and this trip to Kentucky, because he doubted he'd ever come back.

He stirred from his thoughts when Ben slipped into the empty space next to him.

"So, you're gonna take the girl's horses."

It was more of a statement than a question. Parker glanced sideways at the old farm manager. "Yes. That's my plan."

"You know it's gonna hurt."

Ben acted as if he didn't know what to do with his hands, but after a moment of wringing them, he rested them on his knees and studied the ground.

"I didn't make the deal," Parker responded.

"But you're carryin' it out."

It really wasn't the old man's business, but out of respect for the man's age and apparent concern for Reggie, Parker kept silent.

"Four good sales can make the difference between simply surviving next year or doing well enough to not have to struggle. Instead, we're losing all that income."

"That's not my affair," Parker said softly, stifling the stab of guilt he felt. Was this old man playing him? Trying to get him to back down? "And it's not yours either."

"It is," Ben insisted but didn't look up. "I love her. I've loved her since she was a child. Corbin and I took care of her. With her granddaddy gone, she's got nobody else."

"She has a father."

"Pshaw!" Ben spit out the comment and met Parker's gaze. "The man is pond scum. He hurt Corbin *and* Reggie—wasn't even there when Reggie's mom died. Couldn't face it, he said."

Tell us how you really feel, Parker thought.

"I'm sorry," he told the older man. "I'm just doing my job."

Ben nodded reluctantly. "I know. That part's not on you. I just want you to know that losing those four yearlings won't do the farm no damn good."

"I can imagine."

"Not sure you can, bein' who you are," Ben said. He paused to lick his lips. "It's you, though, I'm really worried about."

"Me?"

"And the way she pines after you."

Parker scooted back on the bench to sit up straighter. "Pines after me?"

"You know, cares about you."

"I find that doubtful," Parker commented, wondering if Reggie had said something to Ben about London.

"Oh, she hasn't said anything," Ben came back as if reading his mind. "But she don't need to. I've seen her look at you. I'm old enough to know that look on a woman."

Parker wasn't about to admit anything, not about Reggie and what she'd done with him or to him in London, especially not to this old man. "Look, Ben, the way I see it, whatever is between Reggie and me, now or at any time, is really none of your business."

"I'm just sayin'," Ben replied. "I saw her daddy break her heart. I wouldn't want you to break it too."

"I have no intention of breaking Reggie's heart or any such thing." Parker controlled his anger with effort. "The only thing I plan to do is take the horses that are mine and return to England on Friday."

"You'll cripple Ward Farm," Ben muttered.

Parker's face grew hot. "The way I see it, Ward Farm is building its future on the back of Stuart's Legacy, our stallion. We've had to struggle, too, since the loss of that stallion. I don't think you can criticize my family or me for doing what we have to do. This is a tough business."

Ben stood up and faced him. "I understand you're doing your duty. Just be careful with my girl."

The farm manager left before Parker could think of a rejoinder. Taking a sip of tea to calm himself, he sat back against the bench, his shoulders tense. The conversation had ruined his good mood. Damn the old man for interfering.

Parker frowned. He was doing his duty. Plain and simple.

Just then, he looked up to see Reggie walking toward him, the sway of her hips and the swish of her skirt enticing in a very sexual way. His heart raced.

Damn.

He *was* doing his duty, but at the expense of everything he desired.

CHAPTER TEN

Duty versus desire.

Parker had put his life on hold for years, because doing his duty was important to him. It defined him in many ways. It was how he had been taught. The Eton way. The aristocratic way. Yes, doing his duty had become so much a part of his life that he rarely thought of doing anything else.

But now, he did think of other options as he watched Reggie walk toward him.

Why should Hampton have it all? His brother was the one who should be doing *his* duty, not depending on Parker for help as he always did. Hampton had been bestowed the family birthright. As the eldest son, responsibility for the family should have ridden on Hampton's shoulders. But his brother had none of the mindset needed for the job. In a way, he was like the old king, Edward VIII, who'd abdicated his throne to marry his mistress, a twice-divorced American woman. Hampton wanted his freedom, his fun. Yet, he liked the money that went with the title and estates. There'd be no abdication for Hampton. This wasn't 1936. His brother would have his cake and eat it too. All thanks to Parker's diligence and his penchant for doing his duty.

"What's the matter?" Reggie asked, stopping in front of him. "I'd think a guy, who'd just bought a half million-dollar horse wouldn't have a care in the world." She paused, smirking. "Unless, of course, you can't really afford it."

Parker grinned. Reggie had a habit of goading him, just as he teased her upon occasion. He didn't know many women who had that endearing mixture of shyness and gumption. Maybe that was what he really liked about her.

"The Stuart Racing Stable has the money, luv. Never you fear."

Reggie shrugged. "But what about Parker Stuart? Are you going to buy a nice horse to take home for yourself?"

Again, she amazed him with her knack of understanding his thoughts. She'd gotten it exactly right this time. He waved aside the question. "Be a good girl and stick to your own worries."

She flipped her ponytail and turned away. "I take it you're not so well-heeled on your own. Welcome to the club, Mr. High-and-Mighty."

That stung. Not the lack of money part, but the fact she thought of him as high and mighty. He caught up to her, grabbed her by her arm, and whirled her around. "Look, I'm just doing my job."

He could feel Reggie's animosity even though her damned sunglasses kept him from seeing her eyes.

"And loving every bit of it," she accused.

That had been true. At first. Now, he was conflicted. "You said we are alike. We are, Reggie. Don't you get that?"

"I get it. All too well."

Her posture was stiff. Defensive. He didn't want to fight with her. He had so few days left. Then he'd fly home and out of her life for good.

"Let's get out of here," he suggested.

"Where do you recommend we go?"

"Anywhere but where there are horses."

She recoiled, trying to pull away. "I have work to do at home."

"There's always work." He held her firmly but gently. "Humor me, will you?"

She was so near, so close. It felt so good. If he gave a little tug, she would be in his arms in a split second. He wanted her there, but he wanted them to be somewhere private. He wanted what he couldn't have.

Which was the story of his life.

Her muscles relaxed under his hands, and she glanced over his shoulder at the barn. She shook her head slightly, sighing. "That's just it, Park. I don't know where to take you that hasn't got something to do with horses."

"Then take me to Louisville, so I can see the Ohio River."

"What? You want me to drive you all the way to Louisville? In my truck?"

"I'll put my life on the line to be with you, Reggie."

She leveled her gaze. "Are you kidding?"

"No. Dead serious. I just want us to do something different. Show me part of your state. I'm leaving Friday, remember?"

"Not a moment too soon," she said in a spiteful tone.

Parker chose not to let her goad him. He simply grinned at her then raised an eyebrow in challenge.

"Okay, dammit. Let's go."

Reggie couldn't figure him out. Maybe Ella was right, and Park did like her. Sure. He liked her enough to take her horses.

But that was her father's fault, wasn't it? And his brother's? She should be blaming them for her predicament. Trouble was—she couldn't quiet the emotions rumbling through her heart. They made Park too dangerous to think about. Or to be around.

Driving down Versailles Road, she couldn't escape horse

country. Thoroughbred farms bordered the highway, reminding her of what Ward Farm had once been and what it had now become. She turned onto Interstate 64, toward Louisville, and stepped on the gas. Seventy miles an hour was the speed limit; she drove eighty.

They didn't talk. Reggie couldn't think of anything to say. Everyday chitchat didn't seem appropriate. She didn't want to talk about the horses either. Rod had told her which horses Park had chosen. He'd taken the best she had. All but Jimmy. Park would have taken that colt too, if given the chance. She knew it as surely as she knew it was wrong to hide the horse from him.

Kentuckians who lived outside of the city of Louisville didn't like it too much. Louisville was too big, they said. Of course, those who lived in the city adored it, because it wasn't really too big. It wasn't suffocated by traffic like Chicago or Atlanta. On a good day, a person could drive across the city in thirty minutes. But there was that rural-versus-urban rivalry in the state of Kentucky. Country folks thought the city folks looked down on them. People from Louisville called the country folks "rednecks." So it was tit-for-tat, kind of like Park and her.

It was five o'clock by the time she left I-64 at the Third Street exit ramp. Reggie didn't drive to Louisville much, and being Monday, a workday, there was a lot of commuter traffic, headed luckily in the opposite direction.. She took a right and parked in the multi-storied parking garage under the Belvedere, an elevated space located on the Riverfront and surrounded by high-rise office buildings. Underneath it ran I-64. The Ohio River was on their right as they drove into the garage and so was the fabled Belle of Louisville, an authentic Mississippi river steamboat still in operation.

"You said you wanted to see the river," Reggie said, breaking their silence. "Let's go."

She climbed out of the car and headed up a flight of steps that led into the late-day sunshine of the Belvedere. Park joined her, and they strolled toward the end of the open space where they could look at the Ohio River. They stopped at a guard wall, standing side-by-side. To the west, over the Falls of the Ohio, the sun was starting to set.

"Thanks for bringing me," Park said, turning toward her.

"No problem."

"Thanks for understanding."

She turned to look up at him. "I'm not so sure I understand much."

He shook his head. "You understand more than you know."

"How can that be?"

"Trust me," he said, putting his hands on her shoulders.

She wanted to trust him, but she couldn't.

Park slid his hands down her arms. The feel of his palms on her bare skin made her tingle inside. She took a step back. *No!* Contact with him was dangerous.

But he pulled her back and straight into his arms. With the rumbling interstate traffic and the muddy river far beneath them, they kissed. It was tentative at first, as if he asked her permission. Then it ignited with passion. The hunger of June returned full force to sweep Reggie away. She answered Park's kiss with a full-fledged desire that grew and grew until she thought her heart would burst.

"Oh, I've missed you," she moaned into his lips.

"I've missed you too, luv. You don't know how much."

Had she heard him right? Good grief! What was happening between them?

He broke off their kiss and hugged her tightly against his chest as if he never wanted to let her go. Then his stomach growled.

She really didn't feed him enough.

"Are you hungry?" she asked, snuggled against his fancy Armani jacket.

He brushed the back of her head with his hand, pulling her nearer to him. "I'm famished," he said. "Hungry for you, too."

She ignored that last remark. "If I remember right, there's a restaurant a few blocks from here. We can walk."

"I'd love to."

He let her out of the embrace, and she stepped back, grinning up at him, and held out her hand. "Let's go."

He took her offered hand, and they walked together from the Belvedere onto the sidewalk of Main Street. No words were spoken. She didn't mention the kiss, but she felt its impact in the glow of her heart. She didn't want to think about it. Or lose pleasure of the moment.

They crossed the street and stopped at the Louisville Slugger Museum & Factory with its giant, exact-scale replica of a Louisville Slugger bat leaning against the building. They stared up at the big bat then touched it.

"Think of it as a giant phallic symbol," Park said.

Reggie felt her blush. "Stop it! Don't be crude."

He shrugged, trying to look innocent. "Merely telling it as it is."

"Come on!" she said, tugging him away.

At the end of the block, in front of a boutique hotel and restaurant stood a thirty-foot tall replica of the statue of Michelangelo's David in all its golden, anatomically-correct glory.

"Now, there's a man for you," she jested, hoping to get a jump on him.

"Reminds me of meself, don't you know," Park replied in a fake Irish accent.

"Oh, good grief! Where's your upper crust British modesty?"

"When I'm with you, luv, I've not one bit of humility...or restraint."

He reached for her playfully, but she dodged his grasp.

"I thought you were hungry," she reprimanded. "Let's eat here.

This is a popular restaurant, serving Kentucky cuisine. It's expensive, but you can afford it."

"Ah, you're off the hook for the moment," Park conceded, "but not for forever."

"We'll see about that, mister."

Reggie reached for his hand and pulled him inside the restaurant, where they ordered bourbon and short ribs with locally grown vegetables. They ate, chatted about horses because they couldn't help themselves, laughed, and had cheesecake for desert. They didn't talk about the tension festering between them.

Or what would happen when she took Park home and they were alone again in Richlawn Hall—her home, her heritage...her life.

CHAPTER ELEVEN

Reggie was more than ready for a night of good sex. The kind they'd had in London. Just like she'd dreamed about but had put aside as being too risky. Too scary and misguided. Because for her, good sex meant love, and loving Park was not something she could afford to let herself do.

She wouldn't think about that. She'd just enjoy it and agonize over the consequences later.

But she wasn't ready to see lights burning brightly in a house that should have been dark and quiet. Nor was she ready to find a beat-up Chevy parked in the driveway. Or for her father to be standing at the front door waving his hand in greeting.

"Damn, it's Sam."

"Sam?" Park asked as if he didn't understand.

"My father." Reggie stopped the truck and opened her door. "What in the hell is he doing here?"

"We looked for you at the sale," Sam called down from the porch. "But we couldn't find you. Don't you ever turn on your cell phone?"

"Sorry about him," Reggie said in an aside to Parker.

"No worries. You didn't plan on him being here."

"I sure as hell didn't." Curse words seemed to flow from her lips whenever her father was around.

"You can handle it," Park said. "And I'm right here."

She shot him a puzzled look. What did he mean by that? Was he offering his support? The idea struck her as odd coming from him.

"Thanks," Reggie muttered. "Better get this over with."

She climbed out of the truck and strode to the house.

"Baby girl!" Sam tried to hug her and kiss her cheek when she stepped on the porch.

Reggie pulled away. "What in the hell are you doing here?"

"Don't use that language around me," he scolded. "It's not ladylike. Aren't you glad to see your old man?"

"Not particularly."

Sam ignored her comment and turned to greet Park, who had followed her to the house. "Good to see you, Parker, my man," he said and stuck out his hand.

"Mr. Ward." Park overlooked the hand and nodded politely instead.

Rebuffed, Sam grinned. "Got your horses, I hear. Ben said you picked some good ones."

"No thanks to you," Reggie said with a snarl.

"Don't sound so bitter, honey," Sam came back. "It's a business deal between men."

"Business deal? It was a freaking gambling debt."

She couldn't believe her ears. Her father was a master dissembler. He lied about most things and thought he could charm his way out of the rest. This bet with Hampton Stuart put the end to it. Truly the end. Sam had finally gambled away his stake of Ward Farm. He had only owned one-fourth of the foals that had been born two years ago, and those were now headed to the Stuart's stable.

Thankfully, her grandfather had left everything else to Reggie in his will—the broodmare farm and the produce from it, starting three years after his death. He'd given Sam just enough rope to hang himself with, and from the looks of things, her father had done just that.

"What are you doing here?" she repeated. She knew Sam and didn't trust him one iota.

"Is that any way to talk to your old man?"

He tried glad-handing her, but she stepped aside.

"What do you want, Sam?" At the sound of his given name, he pulled a frown and sobered up, turning away from her.

"Come inside off this damn porch so you can say hello to Denise, your new mama."

Reggie blanched, and the stricken expression on her face cut Parker to the soul. He reached for her, but she was gone, walking ahead of him with her head held high and shoulders squared.

Parker had met Sam Ward in London, and he hadn't cared for the man then. Sam was a crass American, a damn Yank by everyone's book, flaunting his beautiful daughter by his side and playing the role of a wealthy horse breeder. Winning an important stallion like Stuart's Legacy from Parker's foolish brother had given Sam a reputation in racing circles but not a good one. It was apparent the man was nothing but a two-bit gambler. No one had felt sorry for him when he'd lost to Hampton in June. Justice had been served. A wrong had been righted.

At the time, Parker had felt a twinge of sympathy for Reggie. True, she had an embarrassing father, but he didn't seem to cramp her style. He'd taken her to bed that first night because she'd seemed willing enough, and he was certainly able. But something had changed quickly. She was so sweet and funny and generous with her loving and she'd blown his proverbial socks off. He'd had no clue it would happen—hadn't wanted it to happen. The truth was he'd never fallen so hard so fast in his life.

To see the shocked, dead look in her eyes now bothered him more than he cared to admit. After all, he'd come here to right his own wrong. He'd come to seduce her again then leave her like she'd left him. Hurt her like she'd hurt him. But he was finding his intentions had shifted. Parker didn't know what he wanted anymore, but he certainly didn't want to see Reggie hurt.

The entrance hall was cluttered with luggage. Not the leather kind but common polyester carry-ons and wheeled duffel bags. It looked as if they'd come to stay a fortnight.

Reggie stoically followed her father through the dining room, where Parker's painting still lay on the table, and into the kitchen. A bottle-bleached blonde turned from the stove. Waving a spatula in greeting, much as he'd seen Reggie do only days earlier, the woman grinned at them. Thank goodness, her smile wasn't gap-toothed.

"There you all are," she drawled. "We were worried, weren't we, Sam darling?"

She wore Reggie's blue denim apron, but Reggie had looked much sweeter in it than this harsh-looking woman, who wiped her hands down the front of it and came around the island.

"Denise, this is Reggie," Sam said by way of introduction. "And this is Parker Stuart. I've told you about him too."

Reggie stood like a zombie in the middle of the kitchen. Denise caught her two hands and squeezed them. "I've looked forward to meeting you, dear. Sam tells me you're the best daughter in the world."

"Unless he has another daughter I know nothing about, Sam doesn't have anything to compare me with," Reggie replied in a hollow tone.

The cutting remark took the woman aback, but Parker had to give Denise an "A" for effort. "Well, of course, Sam has only one daughter, dear," she said. "He tells me all the time how much you mean to him."

She dropped Reggie's limp hands and turned toward him.

"And you are the handsome, younger brother," the woman cooed, fluttering her fake eyelashes.

Parker knew how to play the upper-class Society card. He nodded his head formally. "At your service, madam."

"Well, yes." Denise turned away flustered and glanced at the only person she could sway. "I almost have the bacon fried, darling."

As Denise returned to the stove, Sam hiked a hip on one of the three barstools pushed against the granite-topped island. "You sure don't keep much food in this kitchen, Reggie. I hope you all have eaten already."

"There's enough for everyone," Denise said, glancing over her shoulder.

"What are you doing here, Sam?"

Reggie's question was quiet, but Parker could tell she was dead serious. There was something in her eyes, a look he didn't like. He was glad she'd never glared that way at him. God help the man who was on the receiving end of her angry stare.

Sam scanned Reggie's face but turned his attention to Parker, "There were some good sales today, pretty high prices, don't you think, Hampton?"

"It's *Parker*," Reggie corrected.

Sam shrugged and turned to Denise. "Hey, hon, did you find any Bud Light in the refrigerator? I could use a bottle right now."

"Not a drop," she said. "This place is dryer than a desert."

"I've asked you several times to tell me why you are here," Reggie interrupted in an impatient tone.

"Why, I wanted to show Denise my home," Sam answered, swiveling on the stool to finally face them.

Parker stood behind Reggie and couldn't see her face. But he could hear the steel in her voice.

"This is *my* home."

"Oh, you know," Sam said with a shrug. "The old homestead. Where I grew up."

Reggie put a fist on her hip. Parker recognized that stance. She had put him his place more than once with that posture.

"The last time you left, I told you not to come back," she told her father. "Not until you changed."

"Changed? Reggie, honey, you can't teach an old dog new tricks."

"I told you not to come back until you stopped drinking and gambling."

"Reggie, honey..."

"Don't you 'honey' me! If you need a beer, you sure as hell haven't quit drinking. Have you quit gambling?"

"Now look here," Sam said. "You can't talk to your old man that way. I'm your father."

Reggie didn't reply to that. Instead she asked, "Why have you really come back? I want to know, Sam."

Her father frowned and seemed puzzled. Parker didn't think she was getting through to him, but Denise had been watching the interchange, standing on the opposite side of the island with her hands on the countertop, and she seemed to understand.

"We met in Las Vegas," she said quietly. "I lost my job, and Sam was kind enough to suggest we come to Kentucky. I've never been to Kentucky."

Reggie eyed the other woman. "Are you really married?"

Denise cocked her head and sighed. "No, not yet, but Sam promises we will be."

"Well, don't count on it," Reggie snapped. She crossed her arms, angrily. "I learned a long time ago that Sam doesn't keep his promises."

"Hey, that's unfair," Sam protested.

"Oh, I'm sorry. I forgot. You keep your promises when they're gambling debts...like losing four of my horses. You *know* you have to keep those promises, but you've never kept a promise to me."

"When did you get so bitter?" Sam asked. "You don't sound like my little girl."

"I haven't been your little girl for a long time."

"Oh, come off it. Don't give me that bull."

Reggie heaved a heavy sigh. "You can stay a few days. There's an extra bedroom upstairs. But you will not make this house your home. This is my home. Granddaddy gave it to me."

"That's fair enough, isn't it, Sam?" Denise asked.

"Sure. Sure," Reggie's father mumbled, but Parker could tell he didn't like it.

"A few days is all we need, isn't it Sam? We can start to get back on our feet. It won't take us long." Denise sounded optimistic and a bit naive.

"And clean up that stuff in my entrance hall before I get back," Reggie commanded, heading for the door. "I've got a horse to look at."

She stormed from the kitchen and through the screened porch, slamming the door behind her. Parker doubted she was going to tend to her horse in her pretty dress and horribly high sandals, but he knew better than to follow her. She needed her space.

Even though she was running away again.

With Reggie gone, Parker felt as if all the energy had been sucked from the room. Denise turned back to the stove, and Sam toyed with a mug of coffee on the counter in front of him. They were like a couple of mannequins in a storefront window. Parker stood silently, waiting.

What should he do now? Finally, without a word, he turned on his heel and retraced his steps to the dining room. There, he gathered up his art supplies and the dried painting of Richlawn Hall and carried his equipment up the front staircase to his bedroom.

So much for his evening with Reggie.

Maybe it was for the best. He had no good reason to go to bed with her again. There was too much potential hurt for both of them.

After all, he was leaving Friday. Leaving for good.

CHAPTER TWELVE

When Parker came down to the kitchen the next morning, he found it empty but trashed, so unlike the housekeeping he'd come to expect from Reggie. A dirty skillet soaked in the sink, and the countertops needed a good scrubbing. But the coffeepot was on, and the coffee was hot.

Reggie had come and gone. He knew where to find her or thought he knew. He skipped the coffee, not wanting to waste time, and left the house through the screened porch.

Would this heat and humidity ever break? Parker was tired of sweating. Tired of the relentless afternoon sunshine.

This morning, the sun was just breaking in the east as he made his way to the barn. As expected, he found Reggie cleaning the stalls with two other workers, including the one he thought was named Juan. Ben wasn't there. Maybe he'd already left for Keeneland and his part-time job.

Reggie glanced at him through the bars of a stall. She didn't say anything, just searched his face with sleep-deprived eyes. They didn't speak. But Parker sensed a connection between them, one that hadn't been there when he'd stepped off the plane in Lexington.

He nodded toward the stall fork in her gloved hands. "Do you have another one of those?"

"In the hay room on the other side of the tractor. There's one hanging on the wall."

She didn't quiz him, but he'd seen the question in her eyes. He didn't explain himself to her and almost couldn't justify his appearance at the barn to himself. He was drawn to her. Wanted to be with her. Knew she needed the help...comfort. That was enough for the moment.

It had been a long time since he'd actually gotten his hands dirty with barn work. Not since he'd left university. Shoveling manure wasn't hard, just never-ending. When the stalls were clean and bedded, a worker climbed aboard the tractor and drove the manure spreader out of the barn, toward a field to spread the manure. With the equipment gone, Juan pushed a cart of hay from stall to stall. Parker joined him and, at the man's direction, tossed a flake or two of hay into each stall.

"Thanks for your help," Reggie said when all the mares and foals were safely inside for the day. "You didn't have to do that."

Parker smiled in response. "I know. I wanted to."

He didn't tell her he had enjoyed the manual labor simply because he was with her.

Park's arrival in the barn puzzled Reggie. What was he doing? Wealthy Brits didn't sully their hands with dirty barn work. But she didn't mind. She was glad to have him there. He'd provided support at a time when she sorely needed it.

What was she going to do about Sam? She'd tossed him out on his rear end, so to speak, soon after their return to Kentucky in June. She'd been fed up with him and his destructive habits. But here he was again, turning up with another unsuspecting victim.

"Are you planning to go to the sale today?" Park asked as they strolled together toward the house. The sun was fully up now, foreshadowing another hot day.

"I'd thought about it," Reggie told him. "I have a couple of yearlings scheduled this afternoon. I'd like to see how they do."

"And it will get you out of the house."

Reggie paused and stared at him. When had Park become so prescient? How could he know that just being in the same house with her father crushed her soul?

"Yes, it will do that," she said, nodding then walked on.

"I need to shower. I'll see you downstairs when I'm ready."

"Sounds great."

Park left her there in the kitchen where she poured a cup of much anticipated coffee. She had to shower and change too. But she was moving in slow motion. After another sleepless night worrying about the farm, her father's antics, and Park's kiss, Reggie found her heart wasn't into much this morning. Gone was her normal gusto for life—her drive to face the day and each problem with a steady determination. At the moment, she felt lethargic. Maybe a little depressed too.

Denise scurried into the kitchen and stopped dead when she saw Reggie. "Darn it. You beat me down here. I was going to clean up this kitchen before you saw the mess."

Reggie took a sip of coffee so she didn't have to say anything.

Denise's lips pulled into a straight line. She ducked her head and hurried to the sink, where she turned on the water and removed a scouring pad from under the sink.

"You know that daddy of yours," Denise said as if making conversation. "When he wants something, he wants it right now. I couldn't put him off last night. Letting me clean the kitchen was the last thing on his mind."

That was more information than Reggie cared to know. She frowned over the rim of her coffee mug.

Denise glanced sideways to see Reggie's reaction. Then she started chattering again as she scrubbed the skillet. "Your daddy's not so bad. He's got a kind heart. If it weren't for him, I'd be a bunch of trouble. He got me out of Vegas just in time. I owe him for that."

Reggie lowered her mug. "You really believe he's going to marry you?"

The woman shrugged. "A girl can dream, can't she?"

Good grief! Denise was much too old to think of herself as a girl. The fact she was counting on Sam to make her life better appalled Reggie. For one thing, Reggie knew her father. For another, the idea that a woman needed a man to complete her and make her happy was totally foreign to Reggie's way of thinking. She'd been taught by her grandfather—and by hard knocks along the way—that she could only depend upon herself. Furthermore, her father's recent gambling losses had made it virtually impossible for her to succeed with the farm. Reggie didn't care what he did with his life, as long as he left hers alone.

"I wish you well," Reggie said. "Maybe you'll have more luck with him than my mother and I ever did."

Denise set the skillet aside to drain.

"Sam still misses your mama," she said, missing the sarcasm in Reggie's voice. "He talks about her a lot."

That was news to Reggie. She straightened her spine and waited for the woman to continue.

"It hurts me to see him grieve. And it hurts me to know he's using his beer and his cards to hide from that pain," Denise said as she dried her hands on a towel. "Many men are like that. They're weak. Most just need the love of a good woman to get through it."

Her mother had used the same word about Sam. *Weak*. Reggie didn't buy it. She could think of other words that better described her father. Manipulative. Cowardly. Jerk.

Denise continued, "He sure is sad about his relationship with you. He's proud of you. You should cut him a little slack."

Anger rolled through Reggie's stomach. She felt her face grow hot.

"Slack? What about me? I was a child when my mother died. If it wasn't for my grandfather, I'd have been homeless. Sam had no consideration for me or my welfare." She gulped a breath. "He was the father, after all. A child is not supposed to raise her father."

Clearly unable to muster a comeback after the outburst, Denise stared at Reggie.

Damn it! Don't cry! Reggie walked to the sink, poured out the coffee, and placed the dirty mug in the dishwasher. She turned to face Denise as she struggled to control impending tears.

"Just keep the kitchen clean, okay?"

The woman gazed back and nodded her head.

Reggie turned and fled up the back staircase just as the first tear trickled down her cheek.

Parker felt better after he'd showered and shaved. His limited wardrobe was a bother, but blue jeans and a blazer were always acceptable to wear in the States. When he came down the back staircase, he found Sam and Denise eating breakfast at the island bar. Sam was reading a Keeneland sales catalog, one of two volumes lying beside him.

"Good morning," Parker greeted them and crossed to the countertop to pour a mug of coffee.

Their reception was cheerful. Denise asked if he'd like a bowl of cereal. "I really need to go to the store for Reggie today," she said merrily. "That is, if we want more food in this house."

"I'll drive you, honey," Sam said.

"Thank you, darling," Denise replied and gave him a gentle kiss on the lips.

Sam caught her by the back of the neck and pulled her toward him, kissing her as if he couldn't get enough.

Ah, domestic bliss. Parker couldn't help but mock them in his mind. They seemed besotted with each other. It was strange to see in a middle-aged couple, so strange he cleared his throat.

"Oh!" Denise pushed away, embarrassed, but Sam returned to his Cheerios and milk as if nothing had happened.

"You mustn't mind us," Denise said. "We can't stop thinking about each other." She blushed. "Or keep our hands to ourselves."

"Indeed," Parker muttered.

Nonetheless, he speculated about the two, especially Denise. Was this how being lovesick appeared? Goofy-eyed and carefree as if no problems existed in the world? She said they thought about each other all the time. Couldn't stop touching each other.

Parker almost choked on a sip of coffee. How was that any different from his attraction to Reggie? In England, he had thought about her constantly. Her leaving him festered until he could think of nothing else. His revenge would be so satisfying. So complete. Reggie deserved it, didn't she? After all, she'd made him fall in love with her.

As soon at that thought popped into his mind, Parker knew he was being irrational. Reggie had not plotted to *make* him fall in love. It had just happened. For both of them, he'd thought. But ultimately, he'd been wrong. He'd been the only besotted one, he reminded himself. Her leaving proved that. He was the only one whose life had changed so dramatically that he couldn't even recognize himself sometimes.

Well, this little internal conversation was certainly an eye-opener.

Parker sipped his coffee, cradling the mug. Reggie wasn't in love with him. He had to be more careful. On guard. Not let himself get carried away. Simply because of long legs, strawberry cream breasts, and a talent for playing on his sympathy.

"Reggie has two of her eleven horses going to sale today," Parker said, making conversation to change the thoughts running rampant in his head. "We thought we'd go back to the sale this afternoon."

Sam looked up, puzzled, from his perusal of the sale catalog. "Eleven? Should be twelve."

"I took four of them, remember," Parker stated.

"She had sixteen head at Culpepper's."

Parker clutched the coffee mug. "You must be wrong. Culpepper himself told me he had fifteen head."

Sam shrugged and flipped through the catalog. "Here it is. Read it for yourself. Scheduled for sale Thursday. 'A dark bay or brown filly by Stuart's Legacy out of American Royal' and 'a chestnut colt by Stuart's Legacy out of Spiritmaker.' Spiritmaker is one of our best mares," he said.

"I don't remember seeing anything out of Spiritmaker at Culpepper's."

Sam grinned at Parker. "Damn me, if the girl isn't a chip off the old block. Has some petty larceny in her just like her old man. Reggie must have sold the colt before you arrived."

"I wouldn't know about that," Parker said in his most polished accent. He didn't like the tone of the man's voice or his implication.

"Ha! Well, I like it! Reggie sold that colt right out from under your nose." Sam was triumphant. "By rights you should have had the pick of the best, and that colt was the best. She screwed you, buddy boy, just like she did in England. And just like I did to your piss-poor brother three years ago when I cheated him out of that stallion."

The man was an ass, an ugly ass. Parker lifted his proud chin and glowered at him. He didn't want to believe what Sam Ward was saying. He didn't want to believe Reggie cheated. He'd check the catalog for himself to be sure. Maybe there was an honest explanation. He'd find out the truth before he let this sperm donor —because father was much too nice of a word to use for Sam Ward—color his opinion of Reggie.

At that moment, Reggie came down the back staircase and joined them in the kitchen. "There you are, Park. Ready to go?"

She was dressed in a black knit skirt with a flouncy hem, a simple white, sleeveless shell, and the chunky sandals. She looked fresh and pretty, and he couldn't help it if his heart turned over in appreciation. Or was it love?

"I'm more than ready to go," he told her, wanting clean air to clear his head.

Reggie blatantly ignored her father and Denise. Parker did too, as he ushered her out the kitchen door.

He hoped Reggie didn't hear the chuckle coming from her father, but Parker did. And it made his stomach sick.

CHAPTER THIRTEEN

"I need a cup of coffee," Reggie said, as she swung the truck into a crowded Starbucks parking lot. "I didn't get my full cup this morning. Too crowded in the kitchen. " She glanced at him. "Do you want something? A pastry?"

"A pastry would be good."

"Want to come in with me?"

"No, I'll wait. You pick out something."

After she parked the truck, she removed her sunglasses. Reggie looked at him, her doe-like eyes expressive. Parker wondered what she was thinking. The trip into Lexington had been quiet. He hadn't felt like talking. Neither had she, apparently. Was she thinking about the previous night and what might have happened between them if Sam and Denise had not shown up? Or was she thinking about her father?

He was. And what Sam had accused Reggie of doing. Cheating. It was a dreadful word. He couldn't believe it of Reggie, but he'd been wrong before about her.

Kissing her fingertips, Reggie reached across the seat and gently touched his cheek. He wanted to catch her hand and draw her across the seat to him. He wanted to kiss her. Full on the lips. But he didn't. He didn't even smile.

Unable to maintain eye contact, she dropped her gaze, retrieved her wallet from the glove box in the console, and climbed out of the truck.

"I'll be right back," she said as she shut the truck door.

Parker sat and let his breathing settle for a moment. Reggie certainly filled a space with energy. She had vivacity, a take-charge attitude toward the world and life. He liked that. For a second, he closed his eyes.

When he opened them again, he reached inside the open glove box and pulled out a notebook. Ward Farm was engraved on the outside, and so was the name *Corbin Ward*. Several times during his stay, he'd seen Reggie make notes in this leather-bound, three-ring binder.

He opened it now. Why not? He needed to learn the truth, if not from Reggie's lips, maybe from her writing. Perhaps this would provide the truth. He shouldn't feel guilty.

But he did.

The binder was filled with information about Reggie's broodmares. Each mare had a page filled with details, such as pedigree, breeding date, time of foaling, complications if any, and more. The pages were written in ink or pencil. Nothing fancy or scientific. Just a breeder's everyday notes about her horses.

Each foal had a page too. He flipped quickly through the binder until he spotted a page for the Spiritmaker colt that had been foaled a year ago. On the page, he read the date the colt went to Culpepper's to be weaned from its mother. The date it started yearling prep was also recorded. Nothing more. No notation of a sale. But this colt had not been presented to him for his inspection. Something was wrong. As much as he didn't care for gambling, Hampton had won the pick of four Ward yearlings. Parker was supposed to see all of them when making his choice.

Reggie had cheated him.

Parker saw through the windscreen Reggie had reached the checkout counter after standing in line for several minutes. He quickly closed the binder and replaced it in the glove box. Then he sat back and shut his eyes. He shouldn't be surprised Reggie had hidden a horse from him. It wasn't a big deal in the whole scheme of things.

But it was. It was a big deal because of what, God help him, he had considered doing yesterday before Sam Ward and his Las Vegas mistress had saved him from making another foolish mistake.

"Well, how's it going?" Ella asked when Reggie sat down beside her. The barn area was humming with activity since the sale started in ten minutes.

Reggie and Ella were too tall to walk and show horses during the sale, so they were often put to work behind the Culpepper's welcome table to greet the guests.

"That's a good question," Reggie answered, watching Park stride away, cell phone to his ear. He'd said he was going to find his agent Jonathan.

"More!" Ella urged. "I need details."

Reggie sighed. What was there to tell? They had kissed, and she had thought they were going home to make love. But her father had shown up, ruining her life once more. That was the sum of how it was going. But there was more, and it had everything to do with the conflicting emotions swirling inside Reggie's head.

"Sometimes I think he cares for me," she said to Ella, "but I know he really came to Kentucky to punish me. He blames me for my father's dealings with his brother. He blames me for taking the

Stuart's stallion."

Ella nodded. "I can see how he might. You're an easy target so he doesn't have to be angry at his brother."

"What I don't understand is how he was so confrontational when he arrived, but now he's so...friendly."

Ella lifted an eyebrow. "And how friendly is he?"

"We've kissed."

"And?"

"And there might have been more... I'd expected more last night...except my dad showed up." Reggie took a breath. "That put an end to it."

"What about today?"

"Sam and his new lady friend are still at the house. But Park's been different."

"How different?"

"That's just it. He's been quiet. Not saying much. I don't know what it all means. What he's thinking. Maybe Sam's arrival showed him what kind of family he'd be getting himself involved with again...if we became close."

"And what about you?"

"I don't know what I'm feeling."

Ella smiled a knowing smile. "Could you be in love with him?"

Reggie acknowledged it with a nod. "I thought I was in London. That's why I left. He doesn't love me, and I can't afford the wasted emotion."

"Can't or won't?"

"Both. It scares me. Do you ever feel like that sometimes?"

Ella sighed. "Are you kidding? I'm scared all the time because I think I'll never find someone to love or who would love me."

"Oh, that's silly. You're selling yourself short."

"But I know myself well enough to understand it's the biggest fear in my life." Ella flashed a self-deprecating smile. "Sometimes,

I wonder if I project some sort of vibe that makes men steer clear of me because I am so needy."

"You're not needy," Reggie protested.

"I'm not like you," Ella disagreed. "I can't go it alone. Honestly, Reggie, I don't know how you do all you do."

Reggie considered Ella's comment, and she sighed, too. "Because I *have* to."

They sat silently a moment. Then a few customers arrived, which put an end to the conversation. Soon afterwards, Reggie's filly left the barn with Ben, headed toward the sales ring.

"Aren't you going to watch the auction?"

"No." Reggie shook her head. "It makes me too nervous. I'll hear about it soon enough."

Her cell phone buzzed, but she ignored it and thought about her conversation with her friend.

At times, it seemed too hard to be strong. Independent. Sometimes, she wanted to curl up in the arms of a man and let him protect her. Let him watch over her and fight her battles for her. But that kind of thinking was stupid. Unless a man had character like Corbin Ward, she couldn't count on him. And Corbin Ward, God rest his soul, was dead. There was no one in her life any more for her to depend on.

Parker Stuart wasn't the one. Their worlds were too different. Where he came from was too frightening. She was too frightened to trust that they could make it together. What if they had made love again last night? What if they had found that same beauty and fulfillment in one another that they'd found in London? Would she ever be able to leave him again?

Her cell phone buzzed again. This time she glanced at it. There was a text message.

"From Sam," she said to Ella and rolled her eyes. "I guess he wants me to bring home a case of beer."

"Better check it."

Reggie did, and her heart stopped.
"Oh, my God, Ella! The barn is on fire!"

CHAPTER FOURTEEN

When Reggie found him standing outside the Barn One complex talking to Jonathan, Parker couldn't believe her panic-stricken news. Tears streamed down her cheeks. She brushed them away with an angry hand movement.

"Will you come with me?"

Of course. She didn't need to ask.

"Let's go," he answered and raced with her to the truck.

He hung on for dear life as Reggie barreled down the motorway, turning onto country roads and driving like a bat out of hell to the farm.

The scene, when they arrived, was out of a horror movie. Two fire trucks from a local fire service stood with red lights flashing near the mare barn. Blue lights strobed from a police car. Men in firefighting gear hovered by the trucks, going and coming toward a smoldering area behind the barn where a shed had once stood. Sam and Denise waited off to the side with several farm workers.

Reggie's truck careened to a stop, and she hurdled from the cab. She ran toward the barn that looked perfectly normal to Parker. Had it really been on fire?

Sam apprehended her, grabbing her by the arm and swinging her around to face him. He held her by both shoulders. "It wasn't the barn. It was the equipment shed!"

"Not the barn?" Reggie sank for a moment against her father.

Parker hurried up to them. "We had word it was the barn."

Sam glanced his way. "I thought it was when I texted Reggie." He turned to his daughter. "Don't you ever answer your cell? Or is it just me you avoid?"

Reggie shook free and squared her shoulders. She ignored Sam's question but asked one of her own, "What happened?"

"One of the workers saw the smoke and called the fire department. Then he ran to the house to tell me. I thought it was the barn. Thank God, it wasn't."

"Thank God," Reggie mumbled, turning to look toward the charred rubble that had once housed her tractor, manure spreader, and a variety of farm equipment. "Thank God, the horses were spared."

She walked toward the barn. Parker followed at a respectful distance, wanting to help but knowing there wasn't much he could do. Instead of circling the barn to get to the shed, they walked through it, down the long aisle way between stalls where Reggie stopped to check on each precious mare and foal.

"I've got to separate them," she said to herself but loud enough for him to hear. "It's time to wean them."

At the open end of the barn, they moved outside and stopped to stare at the remains of the shed.

Parker came up behind her and placed a gentle hand on her shoulder.

She didn't glance back. "The horses are safe. What would I have done if I'd lost them?"

He couldn't answer her question. Instead, Parker gave her shoulder a slight squeeze. Telling her she'd survive, that she'd be okay and rebuild if the unthinkable happened, seemed like so much platitude. It was a cliché he refused to put into words.

"How am I going to replace the tractor?" she asked. "The other equipment?"

Parker didn't know the answer to those questions either. It would be expensive to purchase a new tractor and the heavy-duty manure spreader she needed.

Acrid smoke coiled toward the sky. Hulking, burnt shells of the tractor and spreader remained in the otherwise gray ashes of the wooden building. A couple of firefighters trained a hose on the ruins, spraying it with a steady stream of water.

Sam and a county policeman joined them. Parker withdrew his hand from Reggie's shoulders.

"I'm sorry about your loss, Reggie," the policeman said.

"Thanks, Bob." Reggie glanced at him and gave him a weak smile. "It could have been worse."

"Damn, straight!" Sam said. "Could have lost the main barn. Why haven't you weaned those babies, yet, Reggie? At least they wouldn't have been inside."

Why couldn't the man keep his mouth shut? Reggie chose to ignore his remark, which, Parker thought, irritated Sam even more.

The policeman ignored Sam too. "I'm going to have to bring in an arson investigator, Reggie," Bob said.

"Arson?" Reggie's face paled. "Do you think this fire was deliberately set?"

"We have, for right now, only the observation of the first responders," Bob answered. "When a burning wooden structure produces thick black smoke, it could indicate the presence of gasoline as an accelerant."

Reggie frowned. "I'm sure we kept a can or two of gasoline in the building for the lawn mowers and weed trimmers."

"I understand." Bob nodded. "But the way the fire raced upward through the structure and engulfed it so quickly is suspicious. We need to rule out all other accidental causes, though, before we can call it an arson fire."

"Well, I hope so," Sam said, turning away.

Reggie shook her head. "It doesn't make sense. Who would do such a thing?"

Bob shrugged. "That's what an investigation is designed to find out."

Parker could tell Reggie was distraught. Who wouldn't be with such shocking news? It set up a whole series of questions. Was it one of her workers? Could someone have come onto her property with intent to do harm? What if the mare barn was next?

"What could be a motive for arson, officer?" Parker asked.

The policeman was grim-faced. He answered Parker, but directed a very pointed gaze toward Reggie. "The most common type of arson fire is one set in an attempt to collect insurance money."

An hour later after the firefighters left, Reggie went upstairs to change from her skirt into her work clothes and to call Ben to talk to him in private.

"We'll find a secondhand tractor and a used manure spreader," he said. "We can make do until we can afford new ones. Just be thankful it wasn't the actual barn."

Then he gave her the good news that the little filly had sold for two hundred thousand dollars. To Ben, the glass was always half-full. Having him by her side was a blessing.

After their conversation, Reggie entered the kitchen coming down the back staircase. Ben had tried calming her down, but when she reflected on the policeman's veiled indictment, Reggie's blood began to boil.

"Damn!" She wanted to let out a whole string or expletives. "Bob practically accused me of setting fire to my own equipment shed!"

"I wouldn't go that far, honey," Sam said, looking up from where he sat at the island, side-by-side, with Park. They were both iced tea, having retreated to the cool air conditioning of the house after the firefighters left.

"I'll go as far as I like," she retorted. It took superhuman self-control to tamp down her rage. It didn't help that her father was giving her that "honey" business she hated so much.

"Bob was simply stating a fact," Sam said.

Reggie scowled. "It doesn't take much to read between the lines."

"Well, since you didn't set the shed on fire, you have nothing to worry about," Sam pointed out.

"I say," Park exclaimed in an exaggerated British accent, breaking into the discussion, "putting ice in a cup of perfectly good hot tea is a brilliant idea. You Yanks are certainly wicked when you come to inventions."

What was Park doing? Reggie put a hand on her hip. "I appreciate you trying to lighten things up, Park, but give it a rest."

"Trying to do my bit," he said, gazing at her with concern.

Don't look so worried, Reggie wanted to tell him, but she held her tongue.

She was grateful for her presence. Honestly, without Park in the truck and at the site of the fire, she would have lost it. But she didn't tell him that. Couldn't tell him. Couldn't admit any vulnerability or weakness.

Denise handed her a frosty glass of tea. "I made one for you, Reggie. Would you like a lemon? Some sugar maybe?"

"Neither." Reggie accepted the drink. "Thanks, okay?"

Denise nodded and backed away, going around to the other side of the island. "Okay."

Reggie put a hip on the stool and sat down. She took a sip of tea. An awkward silence filled the room.

"If it wasn't so damn hot, we could sit out in the porch. Corbin used to love it out there," Sam remarked as if he couldn't stand the quiet. "You should enclose that porch, Reggie. Make it a three-season room. I'm sure you can find a contractor that could do it for you."

"And where is the money for it coming from?"

Sam lifted his left shoulder. "Your guess is as good as mine."

So why did you suggest it? Reggie wanted to ask. For heaven's sakes, her father could give a saint a headache.

The landline phone rang. It was located in the entrance hall on an old-fashioned phone table.

"I'll get it," Park offered. "Continue to enjoy your family time."

He got up and went out through the dining room.

"That Brit has his tongue planted firmly in his cheek," Sam grumbled.

"Be nice, dear. Reggie likes him."

Good grief. Was it that obvious? To a woman she'd met only a night earlier? Reggie brought the cool glass to her lips and took a long sip of the iced tea. It was bitter. Just as her thoughts were at the moment.

When Park returned from the phone call, he cleared his throat. Reggie turned to meet his gaze. His brow was wrinkled, but he remained so ruggedly handsome it caused an ache of regret to roll through her heart.

"As much as you dislike the local sheriff," he said with a firm nod, "I believe you'd better give him a call."

"Whatever for?"

Park crossed the room, took the glass from her hands, and

placed it on the counter. He held her by the upper arms, gently, protectively. Seated on the stool, she could look him in the eye.

"Reggie, it was a threat. I think it was real."

Reggie forgot to breathe. When she did, the air escaped through her lips in a whoosh. "What do you mean, Park?"

"A man's voice said very plainly, 'Tell the bitch to pay up or next time it will be the barn.'"

CHAPTER FIFTEEN

Parker was glad Reggie didn't faint dead away. Instead, she pulled herself upright, making herself tall. He'd seen her do this so many times, gathering up her courage before confronting a problem. As he'd seen so many times before, she battled her emotions, trying to curb them to give the impression of strength. He wished she would let him help. He wished he were in the position to do more than simply give her quiet support.

"Who would want to harm me?" she asked plaintively. "I don't understand."

"I do," Denise spoke up.

Sam shot his girlfriend a cautioning look. "Denise!"

"Hush, Sam," Denise told him, suddenly seeming to grow in courage herself. "Reggie needs to know. My problems have already cost her a shed and expensive equipment."

Reggie pulled away from Parker and jumped off the stool to confront her father's girlfriend. "What are you talking about?"

With her hands firmly on the island worktop for support, Denise said, "I'm the 'bitch' in question, Reggie, not you."

"What do you mean?"

"I'm afraid those people are after me. I owe certain people

money back in Vegas. Your father thought if we got out of town, we'd be okay."

"Evidently not," Reggie snapped. She turned on her father. "I'm surprised it's not Sam owing money to those people."

"Oh, no!" Denise raised her voice. "Your father is innocent this time. I know what you think of him—he's told me—but this time, Sam was trying to help me. He was doing a good deed."

Parker knew enough of Reggie's assumptions and accusations to know her life had been so colored by the past she couldn't see the present.

"Tell me, Denise, what trouble are you in?" he asked gently.

Denise's glance conveyed appreciation. "I borrowed money to bury my mother. She deserved a decent funeral."

"And she borrowed it from the wrong sort of loan company," Sam added.

Denise's shoulders sagged. "Otherwise known as the local loan shark."

"Oh, my God!" Reggie spun around, turning her back, as if unable to face the people in the room.

Parker's heart ached for her. He looked back at Denise. "How much, may I ask, do you owe?"

Denise glanced at Sam for confirmation. "I borrowed ten thousand dollars. I paid back some of it and would have paid it all back if I hadn't lost my job."

"But you did lose your job," Parker noted.

Denise nodded her head. "Yes. I believe I owe close to twenty thousand dollars now."

"Twenty thousand dollars!" Reggie pivoted to challenge them. "How in the heck is that possible?"

"Interest," Sam said. "Inflated interest."

"Oh, my God! I can't believe this." Reggie crossed the floor and wagged an accusatory finger at her father. "This is your fault! Why did you bring her here?"

Sam stood up and faced his daughter. "Because this was once my home. Denise is a friend of mine, and she's in trouble. I thought my daughter might have a heart, but it looks as if the only thing she cares about is herself."

Reggie's face reddened, mirroring the pent-up rage she must be feeling. Parker had enough sense to keep silent as she leveled cold, hard eyes on her father. "That is completely unfair."

"Is it? You sold a horse today. You've got enough money to bail us out of trouble."

"And what about the next time?" Reggie demanded. "And the time after that? The money from the sale goes toward making this place a success. It goes to protecting Corbin's dream."

"What about me? What about my dreams? My wants and needs?"

"Your dreams? Your needs?" Reggie stood motionless, as if she couldn't believe what he'd said. "When did our roles get reversed? For heaven's sakes, you're the father. You should be the one caring about your daughter's wants and needs. You should be protecting me."

"Sam." Now, it was Denise's turn to call his name in warning.

But Sam didn't listen. "Corbin! It was always Corbin. You always went to Corbin. Never to me, dammit. *I'm* your father."

"You were never around. Corbin was." Reggie's bleak statement of fact ended the argument. She looked away.

Parker cleared his throat once more. "I don't think blaming each other is getting us anywhere."

"You're right, Parker," Denise said. "We'll leave." She came around the counter and clutched Sam's arm. "Maybe with us gone, those people will leave the farm alone."

"Don't count on it," Sam said with a snort. "They have their sights set on this farm. Unless they get their money, they'll do as they've threatened."

Sam's words were too prophetic to ignore.

"I'll call the police." Reggie said, glancing around.

"That won't do any good. You don't know them." Sam shook his head. "I've dealt with guys like them too many times. They want their money. That's all."

The room grew quiet. The four adults stared at each other, not saying a word. It reminded Parker of arguments in his household. Usually, they were about trouble Hampton had gotten himself into. His mother had always wanted to protect her eldest son, and his father had wanted to string him up by his heels. Parker had always been the odd man out, until he stepped up and calmed the situation with his offers of help. And they'd let him. Even now, Parker could always be counted on to fix Hampton's mistakes. Right his wrongs. Just as in Reggie's case, the roles had been reversed. He'd had to be the big brother protecting a little brother.

Until that moment, Parker hadn't realized just how tired he was of his whole, dysfunctional family dynamic.

Reggie's insides felt like jelly, quivering with so many negative emotions she couldn't separate them. All she knew was that she felt sick and hopeless. Granddaddy had always said 'without hope, a person had nothing.' She had nothing now, facing a bleak future she could neither influence nor control.

Sam broke the silence. "What about that yearling colt you've got down at the old tobacco barn?"

No! Reggie wanted to throttle her father. "What colt?" she asked trying to play dumb.

"There's a colt down in the far pasture, hanging out with that little old teaser. Are you going to take that colt to the sale this week? He's part of Stuart Legacy's crop from a year ago."

Park watched her. He'd know she was lying, know she'd cheated him of consideration for that colt.

"I don't know what you mean," she answered, stumbling over the words.

He father must have sensed he had the upper hand. He grinned slyly at her, as if he'd caught her in her lie. And he had, hadn't he? He'd misrepresented himself so much over the years that her little white lie must have been easy to recognize.

"There must be something wrong with that colt or you'd have him at the sale," Sam said. "Even if there is, you can probably make a few thousand off him, enough to give Denise the money."

Reggie's ears began to ring as her father droned on.

Stop it! He was ruining everything. Once again he was ruining her life.

"We could pay off Denise's debt and get the hell out of here. She has relatives in Atlanta," Sam said. "We'd be out of your hair as soon as we settled up."

Reggie was spinning out of control. Her breathing was short, labored. Slowly, she licked her lips. There was condemnation in Park's eyes. Disappointment maybe. And hurt. Certainly hurt.

"No!" Reggie yelled. "That colt is not for sale! He's mine. He's going to bring the Ward racing stable back to prominence. He's going to restore the farm's fortunes."

"One horse can't do that," Sam scoffed.

Reggie covered her ears with the palms of her hands. "He can, dammit. He's the best colt we've ever bred."

"Then you should have let Parker here have first dibs on him."

Sam's accusation was like an executioner's blade. It cut straight into Reggie's heart, because it was the truth.

She dropped her hands to her side and made fists. She lifted her chin. "Don't you understand?" she asked sadly. "That horse is my last hope. Without hope, I have nothing."

CHAPTER SIXTEEN

Reggie had turned on her heel and escaped once more through the screened porch. Parker watched her go, running away again, running to her horses.

Denise sighed. "I'll go get our things," she told Sam. "We should leave. It may not help, but maybe if they see us leave, they won't bother this place."

"Don't count your chickens before they're hatched," Sam replied. He glanced at Parker. "It's not likely to happen."

Denise touched Sam's sleeve. "All the same, we've worn out our welcome."

Sam nodded as Denise left, heading upstairs via the back staircase.

Parker's legs felt like rubber. He climbed aboard a stool and swirled the ice in his tea. Both men sat in silence, each deep in their own thoughts.

"I've made a lot of mistakes," Sam finally admitted. "Have you ever wanted something, Parker, but never could have it?"

Had he? Sam's question surprised him. Deep down in his heart, Parker knew the answer. He wanted to be first born, the family heir. He wouldn't screw up like Hampton. Then, maybe all that he worked for would be his, not his elder brother's. He didn't need to reply, because Sam didn't expect an answer. The man went right on talking.

"When her mother died, I didn't know what to do. I didn't know how to raise a daughter." Sam swiveled on his stool to face Parker. "Dammit! I mean, how do you handle a girl?"

"I've no clue," Parker muttered. "Women are a bewildering lot."

"That they are." Sam nodded. "Take Denise. She just wants to please. She is so starved for affection that she's vulnerable. Not like Reggie. Reggie can do it all on her own. Corbin raised her that way. She doesn't need me or any other man."

Sam had a way of dropping truth like a bomb. Was Reggie so self-reliant that she needed no one, especially a man? Was it true she didn't even need the likes of him?

Parker had been prepared to propose to Reggie in London. Hell, the diamond ring remained tucked away in his canvas shoulder bag along with his watercolor supplies. Then, she'd walked out on him. Left him. For the farm. For the horses. Those were what mattered to Reggie. Not a relationship—if you could call the hot sex they'd had a relationship.

Maybe that was why she left him. Maybe she didn't *do* relationships.

But the farm was in serious trouble. It didn't take an accountant to understand that fact. And there was nothing he could do about it. He didn't have that kind of money.

Anyway, she wouldn't want his help.

Parker took a sip of tea and came to a decision. He had enough money to pay Denise's debt—to get Sam's girlfriend out of trouble and thereby save the farm, if only briefly. Reggie would hate him for it, but he didn't care. It was his money. He could say he was helping Denise not Reggie, which would be the honest truth, if you didn't dig too deep.

"Let me give Denise the money," Parker said quietly. "I have enough in the bank. Not Stuart Stables money but mine."

"You'd do that for us?"

Parker found it interesting Sam lumped himself into Denise's dilemma. "Yes," he said with a nod.

"Reggie won't like it."

"I know. But let me deal with her."

"Thanks, man. We owe you one."

"Thank me by giving Reggie breathing space for a while. Let her settle down a little."

"Okay." Sam let out a sigh. "We'll visit Denise's sister for a bit."

It crossed Parker's mind that this could be a scam perpetuated by Sam and Denise. God, he hoped not. What a lowdown thing that would be for a father to do. But the man had admitted he'd cheated Hampton. This was going to be a leap of faith, forcing Parker to trust Denise was as genuine and honest as she appeared.

To make the transaction work, Parker would have to draw on the family account that was deposited locally for the sale. He'd pay it back later by transferring his money in Britain to the account. It was no problem, but to give Denise the money, he needed to give her a bank cashier's check.

When Denise heard the plan, she threw her arms around Parker's neck and hugged him.

"I knew I liked you," she said. And then she whispered in his ear, "Don't you dare let Reggie get away!"

Sam packed their car, and they piled into it for the ride to the Lexington bank. When they had the check, Denise called the loan shark and arranged to meet him later that day with the money. Then they returned to the Ward Farm long enough to drop off Parker, leaving him in the driveway.

Alone. Lonely. But for once in a long while, feeling good about his actions.

Storm clouds gathered overhead. Parker gazed up at the gray

sky. He had no doubt his reception from Reggie would be stormy too. But he'd deal with her reaction.

How was it that he'd gone from wreaking revenge on Reggie to wanting to help her in the space of a few days?

Damn! He was such a fool. But the thought of going back home to his same family situation simply struck him wrong. Maybe if Reggie was with him, he could withstand the constant conflict, the shifting emotions within his family. With her by his side, he could live with it.

He wasn't like Reggie. He needed someone. He wanted a relationship. No, he wanted to marry her. That was the honest truth.

Parker shut his eyes and let the wind play across his face.

Ultimately, he didn't blame Reggie for lying to him about the colt. She was desperate, as desperate as he was, but for other reasons. If only he could persuade her to come home with him to England. Ben could watch her farm. They could fly back and forth as needed. Maybe, he could convince his father to put money into the farm. Reggie would be his wife, so his father might listen.

It irritated him to rely so heavily on his family. But what choice did he have? None. The horse industry was all he knew, and without a sizable income, he was stuck working in the family business. His birth order had dealt him a harsh blow, but it was up to him to make the best of it.

He opened his eyes and let out a breath. He needed to find Reggie. She wouldn't be in the house. She would be with the horses.

Ignoring the rolling thunderclouds, Parker topped the crest of the hill behind the house. In the lower pasture, he saw an old tobacco barn. Reggie was standing at the blackboard fence. A leggy thoroughbred grazed in the paddock.

Swallowing his uncertainty, Parker firmed his jaw and strode down the hill.

A stiff breeze rolled down the hill. Reggie turned her face toward it, welcoming its breath of coolness. She saw Park striding down the hill toward her, his expensive jacket slung over his shoulder, his white shirtsleeves rolled up on his forearms. Even in the distance, the man turned her on.

She spun back to the fence and gripped the rough railing. Whatever happened now, she'd face it with the courage Corbin had instilled in her. There was nothing more to be done.

The colt's chestnut body had been burnished by Reggie's hours of brushing. His coat gleamed in the sunshine. She was proud of Jimmy, more pleased with him than maybe any other foal she'd ever produced.

Park stopped next to her. Without a word, he laid his coat across the railing and put his hands near hers on the top of the fence. Together, they watched the yearling graze, flicking away flies with his red tail, his ears twitching from side to side to let them know he was aware of their presence.

"He's got good confirmation in the hind end through his legs," Park said.

Reggie nodded, unable to speak because of the mixture of emotions circulating through her—guilt, pride, anger, even regret.

"He has a balanced, compact body that promises speed," Park went on. "Looks fit, too."

Reggie let out a slow breath and nodded.

"Good job," he said.

"Thanks." She turned to gaze up at Park. "I'll have to take him to the sale tomorrow. He's scheduled for Thursday."

"Why would you do that? This horse is the start of your racing stable."

"Because, once again, I need to bail my father out of the

trouble he's in." She was so furious she could spit. Not a very ladylike emotion, but her father brought out the worst in her.

Park caught hold of her shoulders. His fingers burned through the fabric of her jersey shirt. "That's just it, luv," he said. "You don't have to do that now."

"And why is that?"

"Because I've given them the money. Your father and Denise have left the farm and are delivering the check to their loan shark pals even as we speak."

Her heart did double-time. "You gave them your family's money?"

He gently squeezed her shoulders. "No. I gave them *my* money."

"But I didn't think you had that kind of money? Not your own."

"I had just enough."

What was going on? This was ridiculous. Reggie paused a moment, letting his words sink in. His fingers on her shoulders linked him to her but not in a good way. She was beholden to him now. She owed him.

"Why would you do it?" she asked, doubting he'd done it for Sam.

He must have read her thoughts, because he shrugged. "I did it for Denise. She seems like a nice lady down on her luck."

"I don't believe you," she snapped, pulling away to grip the railing once more. "You did it for me, but why? I cheated you out of owning this colt."

He didn't answer right away. Turning to look at the paddock, his body near hers, Park let her question settle. "Because I could," he finally said.

She bristled, unsure of his intentions. "What does that mean? I lied to you, you know. I'm sorry I did it, but I couldn't give you Jimmy."

"Yes, I know."

The wind whipped up, caressing them with its sudden chill.

"You should be furious with me. Instead you use your own money to help me."

"I'm just that kind of a guy."

There was a touch of good-natured humor in his voice. Reggie had trouble fathoming the whole complicated situation. What became clear within a few heartbeats was that his help meant she couldn't make it on her own. She needed help from others especially Park.

"I'll still deliver the colt to the sale," she said, making up her mind. "You'll get your money back."

"I don't want my money back. I'm satisfied with the four horses I got."

"You'll get your damn money back." Her voice rose. "I'm going to give it to you."

"Fine," he said with a huff of temper. "Give it to me when this colt wins his first stakes race."

"That could be two more years."

"Two years is fine. You'll have to see me again."

"You'd want to see me again?"

He smiled. Then he tenderly removed her sunglasses, lifting them up and resting them on the top of her head.

"Now I can see your eyes," he said.

She frowned at him so hard he laughed. "I like seeing you. Don't you understand?"

She gritted her teeth, studying him. Park seemed sincere. However, her insides smoldered with fear. This was too personal. She didn't need him. She'd left him, and when he arrived, he'd threatened her. He had seemed happy, at first, to take her horses. Now, he was saving her yearling colt so she could hold on to her dream.

He didn't love her. That was the bottom line, wasn't it?

She shook her head. "I still don't get it."

"Then just accept it."

"I can't."

"Can't or won't?"

Ella had asked her the same thing. Reggie wasn't sure she knew the difference. Although she felt like she couldn't accept him at face value, maybe she couldn't because of whatever it was within her that remained afraid of him.

Park could see her eyes now and was watching her. He must be able to see the conflict, the confusion, within her. His soft gaze seemed to say he was reading her soul.

That was even more frightening.

"Look, I understand I should have talked with you first," he said. "I know you don't want charity, and my paying off Denise's debt probably feels like charity. But it saved your farm. That's all I care about."

"We don't know it saved my farm. They could have been lying. Sam could have set the fire himself just to get that money."

Park nodded agreement. "Sometimes, though, we have to trust people are who they say they are. It requires a little faith."

Was he talking about himself? But who was Parker Stuart? And who was he to her? Accomplished lover. Hot, hunky Brit. Aristocratic horseman. Did he have a role to play in her life? She had no clue. Her head hurt just thinking about it.

She looked away. The tension between them was like a live creature. It vibrated. Sang with the wind.

"Do you leave the colt out?" Park asked. "There's a storm coming."

Reggie was glad for the change in topic. "He has access to the barn. He can get out of the rain."

"I hope so. I wouldn't want anything to happen to him."

Reggie grimaced at his words but shrugged them off. "He'll be okay."

"I'm not sure I will," Park said with a grin. "My birthday is tomorrow. I'll be thirty."

"My condolences."

"Thanks," Park replied. "I sure could use a bottle of Guinness to celebrate, though."

"What's the matter? My father's taste in beer doesn't match yours?"

He shook his head, staring across the field. "No. Your father's tastes don't match mine at all. For one thing, if I had a wife, I'd never leave her in her time of need."

Reggie's skin prickled. What did he mean? Was he talking about her mother? About her? Her actions? She chose to ignore the questions spinning around in her head.

Instead, she grinned up at him. "Follow me into the barn then, sir. Our teaser, Mr. Too Little, may have a happy birthday present for you. I'm sure he'll be glad to share his stash."

CHAPTER SEVENTEEN

Why didn't he come out and tell her he loved her?

Because he couldn't. Wouldn't. His pride tripped him up. She'd left him, for bloody sakes. The pain of her desertion burned brightly still. Parker had wanted her to come crawling to him. So, at the moment, he'd just let it be. He wouldn't voice his desires. He'd play his cards as dealt and see what happened.

As Reggie said, the Shetland pony did have a stash of Guinness in the feed room. There were three six-packs of bottled Guinness Draught on a shelf.

"Too Little is my man!"

Reggie laughed, and the mood lightened. "I thought you'd appreciate his horde. We give the pony a bottle each morning with his feed. It's good for his digestion."

"I don't care what he uses it for. I know what I plan to do with it."

"How about ordering pizza for supper? I'm hungry."

"Not much of a cook, are you?"

She gave him a look that said *you should know the answer to that.*

It was his turn to laugh. "I'll be happy to pay."

"I won't let you pay for your own birthday party."

"Okay, you win." Parker was so glad about the atmosphere shift he snatched a six-pack from the shelf. "Tell the pony I owe him a case."

"He'll hold you to it. Now, let's go before it rains."

On the way back to the house, Reggie picked up his jacket and slung it over her shoulder. Parker carried the Guinness as if it were gold. Their conversation, as they ascended the hillside, was normal, everyday chatter about the weather. About how they needed rain. About the horrible, clinging humidity. About how scary the storm clouds looked.

It felt good. So good. Parker's heart hummed. Spending twenty thousand dollars was almost worth it to see the relaxed smile on Reggie's face again.

It was almost like those days in June. When they were lovers and there was nothing between them but good sex.

The pizza delivery guy handed Reggie two hot boxes. She handed him several bills in exchange. "Keep the change."

"Thanks, ma'am."

She turned from the door and kicked it shut with her foot. Park waited for her in the kitchen. It was weird to see him standing there by the island, his smile greeting her return. They'd been nibbling on celery and carrot sticks, food Denise had bought. At least, it made Reggie feel as if she was getting her daily dose of vegetables. Besides, chatting with Parker had been fun. A little like old times.

Old times? For them old times was less than three months ago in London. When the owners of Stuart's Legacy had come to town, the Stuarts had wined and dined them. Reggie could see now that Hampton had probably planned to win the stallion back in another poker game. She had to give it to her father that he had never put the stallion on the line during those games. Tragically, the horse's untimely death made his behavior a moot point. Park, she guessed, had been tasked with keeping her occupied and away from her father, because she would have put a stop to his wild, erratic behavior.

In the end, she'd lost her heart much too quickly and unwisely. Meanwhile, Sam had lost four of her yearlings. At the time, Reggie had thought Sam's loss was worse, a betrayal of the family. She still thought that. But standing in her grandparent's kitchen, seeing Park there, made her realize Ella might be right. Maybe she did love him.

A lot of good it would do. He was still leaving town on Friday. So far, she hadn't heard about any change of plans.

Park lifted the boxes from her hands. "Let's not eat in the kitchen."

She looked around. "You're right. The ghosts of Denise and Sam haunt the kitchen."

"Let's eat on the porch and watch the storm."

Reggie liked the idea. "I'll get plates and napkins," she offered.

"Don't forget the Guinness."

Park had put the boxes of pizza on the table and opened them by the time she joined him.

"I got the works and a simple pepperoni and cheese. I wasn't sure what you liked."

"At the moment, I'll eat anything."

The way he looked at her when he said that was provocative, as if he was referring to her. She smiled to herself. She wasn't opposed to giving him a going away present. A birthday present, too. A night together would wrap it all up neatly and tie it with a bow. It would end their relationship on a good note. No regrets.

"Here," she said, handing him a plate. "Get started."

His gaze connected with hers as he took the plate from her hands. "Thank you, ma'am."

"That's the second time I've been called 'ma'am' tonight," she told him. "Makes me feel old."

He laughed. "You're not old. I'm the one turning thirty."

"You don't look thirty."

"I don't feel thirty."

"Because you're not—yet."

"Lovely point. Thanks for reminding me."

Reggie loved bantering with him. She'd forgotten they used to do it. She'd forgotten so much about that time in London. Maybe she wanted to forget it. As she picked up a piece of pizza and placed it on her plate, she realized forgetting was a defense mechanism to hide the hurt. The fear.

She didn't want to be afraid tonight. She wanted to give Park that birthday gift. In many ways, she needed it herself. The connection. The bonding. Good sex was one thing, but there was more to it than that, and that was what she wanted.

Maybe she could fool herself into believing she could have it with Park, even for a night.

Park piled several pieces on his plate. "Let's not eat at the table."

"You're feeling rebellious tonight."

"I'm in America. Casual dining is accepted."

Reggie grinned at his comeback. "You're right."

Park took his plate of pizza and a bottle of Guinness to one of the two wooden, plantation rockers that faced the fields. There was a side table between the chairs where he set his bottle. Reggie joined him, taking a seat in the second chair and put her bottle beside his. The ceiling fans rotated slowly overhead.

"Now I know why Mr. Too Little is so happy to have his morning mash," she said between bites.

"Guinness is one of the pleasures of the British Isles."

Reggie took a sip from her bottle. "Just one of them?"

"We have a long and proud heritage," he said in his exaggerated, high-falutin', British accent. "Part of it is our billion dollar brewery business."

She couldn't let him outdo her. "Well, Kentucky is known for its beautiful women, fast horses, and good bourbon."

"Are you sure it's not fast women and beautiful horses?"

"Oh, you!" She wanted to throw a pepperoni at him but thought better of it.

The first drops of rain began to fall.

"That should settle the dust," Park remarked.

"Yes. We really need a good soaking."

They rocked, ate pizza and sipped beer, letting the sudden rush of cool air envelop them. The days were growing shorter, and the falling darkness was made darker as the thunderclouds rolled in.

"I should turn on the porch light," Reggie said.

"Leave it off. I like the dusk and watching the storm."

Reggie rested her head against the back of the rocker. The tension she'd felt upon his arrival, the antagonism, was gone. It was amazing. Almost unbelievable.

A sudden clap of thunder made her jump.

"Careful," he warned. "Don't spill any of that good beer."

"Your priorities are mixed up," she came back. "Don't you have any consideration for me? That scared the heck out of me."

"I have plenty of consideration for you, Reggie," Park said softly. "More than you know."

His words sent a thrill through her. In the dim light, she could see the gleam in his eyes, the tiny smile on his lips. His words also changed the tone of the evening. Playful banter ceased. There was seriousness to his bearing, in the way he turned from her and took a bite of pizza as if to distract his thoughts.

Oh, Park. I want you so much.

She couldn't put her thoughts into words. Maybe she didn't have to. Maybe her eyes, unprotected by her sunglasses, gave her away. For tonight, she hoped it did.

There was something to be said for having good sex, especially with the man she loved.

CHAPTER EIGHTEEN

"I am so full," Reggie said as she rocked in her rocking chair. "I feel as fat as a dog tick."

Parker grimaced. "Lovely simile," he said. "But you thankfully don't look like a dog tick."

"Thanks for the compliment."

"No problem. In fact, you're one of the most beautiful women I've ever met."

"Now, that *is* high praise."

"I mean it, Reggie."

Night had cloaked them. Only occasional flashes of lightening illuminated the porch, but it was enough to see the faint outline of Reggie's smile. He didn't want to want her. But he wanted her so badly he could taste the desire. How could he convey this longing without scaring her away?

The wind changed at that moment, blowing rain toward the porch, showering them.

"That ruins a lovely evening," he said standing to gather up the boxes of pizza. "We'd best go inside or get soaked."

She agreed and helped him pick up the dishes and bottles. They scurried into the kitchen. After being outside in the dark, the room was bright and dazzling. Reggie had bagged the leftovers and was sticking them into the refrigerator when the lights flickered.

"Oh, no!"

He glanced at her just as the lights flickered again and snapped off. It was pitch black.

"Doggone it. Lost power. It happens all the time," Reggie said.

"I love your American expressions."

"Well, I can think of harsher things to say at a time like this, if you'd like me to. Maybe a few 'hells' or 'damns'."

Parker felt his way around the counter to where she stood beside the refrigerator. "'Doggone it' is just fine."

He drew her into his arms, and she came to him. She didn't resist him as he'd thought she might. Parker kissed the top of her head. Her hair smelled like the out-of-doors, like horses and vanilla and pizza. An enticing combination.

"I was wondering how best to do this," he admitted into her hair. "How to kiss you again and make love to you."

She threw back her head, trying to see his face. "You could ask."

"I was unsure of my reception."

"I sort of assumed this would happen last night, except Sam and Denise showed up."

Last night and the events of the day seemed so far away. Only this moment existed. He couldn't speak. He simply held her, feeling her warmth, her heartbeat.

Parker had wanted her to beg for his lovemaking. Instead, she was inviting him. Making it possible for him to achieve one of his goals of the trip, but not in the way he'd planned. Not with anger and hostility. But with tenderness, and yes, his unspoken love.

Suddenly, he clasped the back of her head and crushed her mouth with his lingering, devouring kiss.

"It's been so long," he groaned into her lips.

They'd kissed yesterday, but not like this, not with pent-up passion building with each tortured breath. He'd make love with her then he'd ask her to marry him. To return with him to England. To be his wife.

She reached up and touched his cheek. "In the old days, before electricity, a man and a woman went to bed when it got dark."

"Is that an invitation?" he asked. She nodded, and he clutched her to him, almost fearful she'd disappear on him again. "I'm afraid I am not like your American Rhett Butler. I don't think I'm strong enough to pick you up and carry you upstairs."

"Rhett Butler is fiction."

"But you Yanks love romance."

"Thanks to you Brits and your Mr. Darcy and Mr. Rochester."

"Of course." Parker kissed her again. Flashbacks of long nights together tumbled through his head. "Perhaps, then you can show me the way. My room is at the head of the stairs."

She giggled. "Come with me then."

Reggie grabbed his hand and pulled him around the island. They stole carefully across the floor. At the door to the back staircase, she paused. "You're sure?"

"If you are." There was indecision in his husky baritone voice.

"I'm fine with it, seriously."

"I'm glad you are."

It was strange to talk so politely about having sex. The niceties hadn't bothered them in June. But tonight was different. He had his plans. He had his ring. The uncertainties of past events left him without his characteristic cockiness, especially with this woman, because so much counted on tonight.

"Watch your step." She pulled his hand again, and they slowly mounted the stairs.

At the top, occasional flashes of lightning showed through the hall windows. Reggie led the way to his shut door. She opened it, and they entered the room one after the other. Once there, she turned to face him.

No words were spoken. In the dark, they felt their way with each other. Reggie reached up and unbuttoned his shirt, one at a time, with a tantalizing slowness that started to kill him. He let her take the lead, because this was what he'd intended when he came to Kentucky. He wanted her to seduce him. To want him. Now, it was happening, just as he'd dreamed. Reggie stood so close, her fingers brushing his chest. It rose and fell with his tortuous breathing.

When she finished with all the damn buttons, she released the one on his blue jeans fly. Then she tugged on his shirttail, pulling it from his waistband. The cool air felt good on his heated skin. He helped her by tugging off the shirt and dropping it to the floor.

"My turn." Parker released the buttons of her top. Then she raised her arms and lifted it over her head.

He saw only her shadow but touched her bare shoulders with both his hands. Her skin felt so smooth. He traced the bones of her neck until he reached her chest and her bra. There, he opened the front clasp with a quick flick and tossed the bra to the floor.

"I forgot how experienced you are," she said, her voice thick with desire.

"I haven't been with anyone since you left."

What made him admit that? Did he want her to understand how much her leaving devastated him? How much she'd meant to him?

He touched a breast, feeling her nipple harden. Bending, he took it into his mouth. More than anything in his life, he knew he was home. Where he should be. With the woman of his heart.

"Oh, Park," she gasped. "I've missed this."

This. But not him. He'd take the simple admission. For the moment, it was enough.

His hands shaking, he slid them down her hips, feeling the

rough denim fabric covering them. Then he unzipped her zipper, tugging, cajoling the jeans down to her knees. Dropping to his knees, he kissed the thin gauze of her panties. He grasped her hips, drawing her to his mouth. She groaned as he slipped the panties down a fraction, kissing her, using his tongue, inviting her to climax.

She came quickly. Standing in the dark with her clothes around her work boots, the rest of her luscious body naked, she clutched his shoulders, her nails biting into his flesh. He didn't care. He rejoiced in the quiver of her muscles as she surrendered to him, as he felt her quick release. Had she been waiting for this moment?

"Oh, my God," she murmured. "My knees are weak."

He scooped her into his arms then and placed her gently in the middle of his double-sized bed. "There you go, Rhett Butler style," he said.

"My romantic hero." A flash of lightning revealed her playful smile.

Parker unlaced her boots and tugged them off. Then he drew off her jeans and panties down her legs and over her feet until she was completely naked. Ragged lightening illuminated her. Reggie lifted a hand toward him, leaving it suspended in the air as a gesture of invitation. She lured him with her smile, with the taut contours of her athletic body. His body throbbed with pent-up hunger. Only this woman had the power to make him love and lust. If she only knew of that power, he'd be in big trouble.

Turning quickly, Parker dispensed of his own clothes and shoes. He expertly donned protection then returned to her. The mattress shifted and sank as he joined her. His knee grazed her hip. His breathing was unsteady, harsh; his movements, shaky. Gently, he stroked her skin then moved his hand down her belly. Her curls were wet with his lovemaking. He touched her there again, and she arched, rising to meet him.

"Park!" she called his name. "Parker!"

Her use of his real name threw him over the cliff. "Oh, God, Reggie!"

She reached for him, touching his upper arm, her movements beckoning. He swung his leg over her hips, balancing above her. He rubbed against her belly, pulsating with need. Resting his weight on his elbows, he kissed her. The poignancy of the kiss wasn't lost on him, even in that moment of intense passion. It was as if she poured out her soul in the kiss. He answered her, trying to speak his love in the silent mouth-to-mouth caress, the only way he knew how.

She grasped him and moved him into her. The shock of her warmth reverberated throughout his body. He remained still, savoring it, but growing feverish with each heartbeat. Then pure animal instinct took over.

"Reggie!" he murmured and moved within her with slow strokes.

Was it his imagination or did the thunderclaps and lightning flashes crescendo with his climax?

With the pouring rain outside, he rejoiced in his release. He delighted in Reggie. And as they had done in June, they made love again and again until they both fell to sleep exhausted in each other's arms.

CHAPTER NINETEEN

Reggie awoke to an afterglow of lovemaking. It was late. Later than her normal five o'clock rising time, but sleeping in felt good. Waking up with Park beside her felt just as marvelous. She glanced over at him and smiled. He smelled musky, like their night of passionate sex, and he was curled into a fetal position facing her. One hand rested on the mattress as if it reached toward her.

Not now, buster! She had to take care of something. With a self-satisfied smile on her face, she swung her legs off the other side of the bed and stood, giving herself the luxury of a long stretch. Then she padded, naked, out of the bedroom, across the hall, and into her bedroom where she visited her en suite bathroom.

When she returned, the bed was empty—its rumpled sheets testimony to their lovemaking. Reggie smiled, remembering. The toilet flushed. Water ran in the sink. Park emerged from his bathroom with a grin on his face.

"Good morning, beautiful."

"Good morning yourself. How about breakfast? That is something I can cook!"

He walked around the end of the bed and caught her in his

arms. "I'd love breakfast." He kissed her. "In fact, I'd love another taste of you."

"Not on your life! I've already slept too late."

"Ah, you're a hard mistress."

"And you, sir, are greedy."

He crushed her to him, kissing her. The place where he'd tormented her all night came alive.

"Oh, Park," she groaned.

Before she knew it, Reggie was amidst the rumpled sheets crying out Park's name as they both climaxed together.

"I guess that's what's called a 'quickie,'" she gasped after he scooted off and collapsed by her side, his arm possessively resting across her waist.

"I believe it is."

His breath was ragged. Sweat glazed his body. She touched the web of dark curls on his chest. "If you stay around any longer, I'll never get any work done."

The remark was spontaneous. After the words left her mouth, she realized what she'd said.

He pushed up on his elbow, resting his cheek on his hand. He gaze searched hers. "What if I took you with me?"

"Why would I go with you?"

"As my wife."

"What?" Reggie sat up quickly. Fear spiked through her. "I can't be your wife."

Park looked up at her from his reclining position, seeming not bothered by her sharp refusal. "I was going to ask you to marry me in London," he said dispassionately, "but you ran out on me."

In disbelief, she stared down at him. A faint sigh escaped her lips. "I had to go home. Stuart's Legacy had died."

He touched her arm. "I know." Turning over, he climbed from the bed and walked buck-naked across the floor to a chest of drawers. On top was his messenger bag. When he came back, he held a black velvet box. "I even had your ring."

Was he kidding?

He stretched out a hand, opening the top of the little box. "See?"

"Oh, my!"

The ring was gorgeous—a large round diamond in a square, four-prong setting with a small diamond at each prong. It looked old and very, very expensive.

"It was my grandmother's," Park said. "My American grandmother. She left it to me when she died."

"Oh, Park, it's beautiful!"

"The center diamond is two carats, I believe." He took the delicate ring from the box and turned it so she could see the setting. "This part is platinum, and it's hand-engraved."

He looked so proud. Reggie had never seen him like this. It was a far cry from the cocky guy who'd first stepped foot on her farm. He was excited. Vulnerable. Scared. Almost child-like.

"I remember my grandmother wearing it," he told her. "She was very much like you."

"I doubt that." Reggie dismissed his comparison with a shake of her head. She looked away unable to meet his eager gaze.

"She was independent and stubborn," Park recounted. "She gave my grandfather a run for his money. He was fond of saying his Yankee wife challenged him every day, from the moment he awoke to the time she let him go to sleep at night."

Park smiled. Reggie was tempted to reach out and touch his arm. To indicate she understood his feelings. But if she touched him, she was likely to yield to him and his dazzling, boyish smile. She was likely to draw him back to her and make love to him again. She couldn't afford to do that. Where Park was concerned, she was like an addict, never sated. That's the reason she had left him. With him, she lost control.

Besides, she couldn't marry him. It was plain crazy.

To regain command over the situation, she went on the offense. "I expect you'd want me to move to London with you."

His eyebrows furrowed. "For the time being. It's the only way."

"There's no way I'm moving anywhere," she put it bluntly. "I'm not leaving my farm."

"I thought Ben could care for it." His reasoning was indecisive as if he was feeling his way. "Until I am able to divest myself of my family responsibilities, I am unable to live with you in Kentucky."

"And I have no family responsibilities?" As the anger rolled through her, Reggie felt suddenly vulnerable. She lifted a corner of the sheet and pulled it over her, hiding her body, covering her breasts.

Her action wasn't lost on Park. He placed the ring back in its little box and returned it to his canvas bag. He walked back to the bedside unashamed and stood looking down his aristocratic nose at her. Park was a magnificent man with a splendid physique. The term "eye-candy" came to mind.

"Did I mention that I love you?" The way he asked it was off-handed, as if he'd just recognized the fact or decided to tell her.

"Not lately," Reggie replied, not believing him. "It's not like you to toss around the 'love' word."

"I knew in London," he said, "but you ran away."

"I'll never live that down, will I?"

He waved his hand toward the rumpled sheets. "We're good at this," he said, "but you evidently don't feel the same way about me as I feel about you."

She stared back at him unable to make sense of what he was saying. Unable to straighten out her mixed up emotions.

"I'll not beg you, Reggie. Either you love me enough to come home with me as my wife, or that's all. I'm done. I'll be gone as soon as I can catch a ride into Lexington."

"Are you for real?"

When had all this love stuff come up? Only yesterday, she had been worried about Sam and his shenanigans. Simply put, Park was a guy who attracted her, who was good in bed. She had a brief history with him. But marry him? That was far from her mind. Far from his too, she'd thought. He'd set out to ruin her horse farm. He was still ruining her horse farm. Not much had changed except she'd made love with him all night long, losing control of herself. Of the way she wanted to be.

Bottom line, her grandfather would be ashamed.

He stood ramrod straight. Like a regal prince. For a brief second, Reggie longed to toss off her sheet, toss away her misgivings, and spring out of the bed into his arms. But Park was giving her an ultimatum. One she couldn't accept. That wasn't the basis for a good marriage, not in her mind.

"Fine," she said. "I'll ask Ben to drive you into Lexington."

"So, that's your answer?"

"Yes."

They gazed at each other in silence as if neither of them could believe the finality of her one word. In the entrance hall, the grandfather clock bonged the half hour. Was that a sign from her grandfather? Did he approve of her refusal?

More to the point, could she live up to the expectations she put on herself, expectations that she felt came from Corbin?

Park broke eye contact and turned away. He reached down and pulled on his boxer shorts. "If you don't mind, I need to shower and change."

"Fine," she said, dropping the sheets and proudly climbing from the bed.

He turned and gazed at her. She let him view her nakedness, lifting her chin with dignity and determination.

Then the doorbell rang. Someone beat on the front door with what sounded like a fist. Fear sprang into Reggie's heart.

Park pulled back the window curtain and looked out the window. "I can't see who it is, but I see Ben's truck outside."

"Something's wrong."

"You wait here," Park told her. "I'll go." He scooped up his blue jeans and jerked them over his hips.

Reggie watched in panic as Park strode out of the bedroom. She heard his bare feet thump down the front staircase. She held her breath as he opened the front door.

CHAPTER TWENTY

Ben was at the front door. He was grim-faced, covering his surprise with a frown. "Where's Reggie?"

"She's upstairs," Parker told him.

The old man knows what we've been doing.

It was quite obvious, really, with him standing in the door shirtless, barefoot, and wearing only his jeans.

"I need to speak to her."

"Come in. I'll get her for you."

"I'd rather stay outside."

Didn't the farm manager want to be in the same room with him? "What's wrong, Ben?"

"That's between me and Reggie."

Parker bit back an angry retort. Of course, Ben wouldn't talk to him. He was the interloper. The British guy who had taken Ward horses. The guy Ben had warned not to harm Reggie.

At that moment, Parker heard her clomping down the staircase. He turned. She was fully dressed even down to her work boots. Anxiety clouded her eyes. Parker knew she was scared. Whatever news Ben had wasn't good news. It didn't take a psychic to figure that out.

She came up behind him, crowding him at the door. "What is it, Ben?"

"I can't tell you here, Reggie." The man's words were soft, tense. He glanced up at Parker as if signaling he couldn't talk in front of him. "It's about Jimmy."

"He knows about Jimmy," Reggie said. "Sam told him."

Ben looked confused then nodded. "There's no easy way to tell you."

Reggie touched Parker's back as if bracing herself. "Tell me."

"He's dead."

"Dead?" The tone of Reggie's voice was dead with disbelief. "How?"

"A lightening strike."

Reggie wavered, resting a split second against Parker's shoulder. "Oh, my God!"

"I thought the horse had access to the barn." Parker supported her with his arm around her waist.

"He did." Ben glanced at Parker. "I suppose the storm came up too quickly. Juan found him outside near a tree."

"I should have put him in his stall."

"Reggie, you didn't know about the storm," Ben said. "You can't blame yourself."

"I can." She pulled away from Parker, standing straight. "I knew the storm was coming. I had other things on my mind."

Did Ben guess what she meant? Parker knew. He had been on Reggie's mind. The old man glared at him as a wave of guilt hit Parker. No! He would not feel guilty. A lightening strike was an accident. Many horses were lost that way. It was one of the risks of the business. It was something a horse owner had to accept.

"Take me to him," Reggie said. "Please, Ben."

She looked to be in shock. Parker reached for her, but she pulled away again. "I'll go with you," he offered.

"No! I want to go alone."

Not looking back, she left the porch and climbed into Ben's pickup truck. Ben went around the front of it. When he reached the driver's side, he paused and leveled a hard gaze at Parker, full of anger and condemnation. Ben blamed him. Parker tried not to blame himself.

He imagined how Reggie felt. It must seem to her as if another nail had banged into the coffin. She'd counted on the yearling to bring her farm back to prominence. Parker would be sick, too, if he'd lost a promising colt. Sick with grief for the loss of life, not to mention the potential he'd seen in the horse.

Yet, why wouldn't she let him help her? At least, let him comfort her during this difficult time?

Parker shook his head, resigned to the situation. He'd spent enough time after Reggie left London being angry, wanting to seek revenge. Not knowing had been the worst part. Now he knew what she felt about him. The reality was somehow easier to handle than the limbo of half-hope.

With heavy steps, Parker went back into the house and shut the door. He ascended the staircase and went into his bedroom. Evidence of their night of lovemaking was scattered about in his pile of clothes on the floor and especially in the messy sheets on the bed he'd once thought too small for the job. He'd been wrong, as he'd been wrong about many things in his life. Family loyalty was one of them. But it was all he knew. His foundation. His purpose.

Resigned to the way things had turned out and with a fatalistic view of his life, Parker grabbed the top sheet. He pulled it up to the headboard, straightening it. Like his American grandmother had taught him, he made the bed. When he was finished, it was crisp and neat. No one could tell what had happened in it earlier. No one could read the telltale signs of making love.

Then Parker showered and dressed. He packed his leather

luggage and brought his belongings downstairs, leaving them in the entrance hall.

He was in the kitchen putting on a pot of coffee when the ringtone on his iPhone sounded. Pulling it from his pocket, he checked the display. His mother. *Wonderful.* But he took the call, because that was the kind of son he was.

"Parker, darling, how are you? Happy birthday."

It was his birthday. He was thirty. He didn't feel like thirty— more like thirteen after his first breakup.

"Thank you," Parker answered.

"You don't sound well, darling. Is anything wrong?"

"No." Just his whole life was in ruins.

"Oh, hold on a minute. Your father wants to talk to you."

Parker pictured his parents fighting over the phone in the paneled library. They didn't like mobile phones, preferring a landline.

"Why did you spend twenty thousand dollars?" The elder Stuart's voice was brusque.

He came right to the point, didn't he? Parker let out a silent sigh, being careful not to make noise. "I'm taking care of it today, Dad. I'm transferring money from my bank account into the stable account."

"But why did you need that kind of money?"

"It's personal."

"Personal? Does it have something to do with that Ward woman?"

Parker didn't like his father's tone of voice.

"No," he answered. "It doesn't." He didn't add the word "technically" because the money had, in a way, been for Reggie.

"I don't like you borrowing money like that. It's too much like your brother."

Comparing him to Hampton Junior was rubbish. He and

Hampton were night and day. That his father could make the association offended him.

"I plan to pay it back," Parker said controlling his voice. "With all that's been going on, I haven't had a chance."

"That Tiznow colt seems promising," Hampton Senior said, changing the subject in a dismissive way. "But I'm not sure I would have paid that much for him."

Parker gritted his teeth. How he longed to suggest to his father that he should have come along on the trip and done the bidding.

"Those offspring by Stuart's Legacy look to be out of inferior stock. Are you sure you picked the best of the lot?"

"Yes, I picked the best."

He refused to mention the best yearling had been killed in a freakish accident. He'd never tell his father that tidbit of information. In fact, he resented his father's cross-examination and lack of trust. For a split second, Parker questioned his family loyalty. His family pride. Why not chuck it all and live here in America with Reggie. They'd be poor, but happy.

Because Reggie didn't want him.

He'd admitted his love, and she'd rejected him. What more could he do? Like he told her, he wouldn't beg.

It was horses first with Reggie. He needed to remember that.

"Okay," Hampton said, distracted. Then to Parker he said, "Your mother wants me to tell you happy birthday."

"Thanks."

"When will you be coming home?"

"Friday."

"Okay. Your mother wants to talk to you."

"Fine."

"Happy birthday, son," his father repeated.

"Thanks."

"All your father wants to do is talk business," Parker's mother complained when she got back on the call. "He forgot to tell you the most important thing."

Parker looked up at the kitchen ceiling. "What's that?"

"You turned thirty today, Parker."

"I know, Mum."

"Well, you'll have your inheritance now."

Parker pulled the iPhone from his ear and stared at it. Then he put it back to his ear and asked, "*What* inheritance?"

"My mother, dear, your grandmother, left all her money to you."

"What?"

"You were named 'Parker' after my family," his mother said, as if chatting with her lady friends at tea. "My mother always said you were her favorite, because we spoiled your brother so much someone had to favor you. You don't remember her, because she died when you were so young."

"But I do remember her," Parker replied. "I remember coming to her house in Virginia and going to Disney World. When I turned twenty-one, you gave me the ring she left me."

"Good, gracious, darling. She left you more than a ring. She left you her whole estate."

"What?" It sounded improbable. Fantastic. "How much is her estate."

"I don't know, dear." Parker could hear her talking to his father. "Your father doesn't know the details. He says it's her house in Virginia and the farm. There's a good bit of money too."

His heart raced. This was brilliant news, even though it had only started to sink in. "Why would she leave it to me?"

"Well, dear, she said it wasn't fair your brother inherited all the Stuart money. She thought it was very 'old school' she said. So, there you have it."

"But why didn't I know about it? Why didn't you tell me?"

His mother sighed loudly. "It was your father, darling. He didn't want it to ruin you."

"Ruin me?"

"Yes, like he says money has ruined Hampton."

Bitterness crowded out all his newfound excitement. "I'm not Hampton."

"Well, of course not, darling. But you know your father. When he takes an idea to heart, there's no dissuading him."

"I know."

"And you've been such a help to Hampton over the years. We were afraid if we told you, you'd forget your devotion to your brother."

That was the unkindest cut of all. When had he ever forgotten his allegiance to the family? By God, that's all he had.

"It's a wonder you decided to tell me now," he said with a sarcastic huff.

"Oh, no, dear. We had to tell you now. You turned thirty. The money is yours when you turn thirty."

"I guess I'm a rich man." His voice was caustic. Resentful.

"Well, of course, you are, darling. A very rich man."

CHAPTER TWENTY-ONE

Ben drove Reggie back to the house and stopped at the front door. The last few hours had been the worst of her life. Well, almost. Watching her mother die had been the worst.

Yet, seeing her little yearling, lifeless in the field, held a special poignancy for her. The horse had been her big hope for the future. Spiritmaker was in foal again to Stuart's Legacy, but it would be two years before the foal was old enough to go to the sale—that is if it was a live birth. So much could happen to a horse from conception to foaling. And after that, nothing was assured. Like a chance lightning strike. Like being in the wrong place at the wrong time.

"Do you want me to wait?" Ben asked, his gaze filled with compassion.

"Yes." She smiled bravely. "Let me see what Park plans to do. He said he wanted to leave and needs a ride."

"I'll wait."

Reggie left the truck and shut the passenger side door. She walked the few steps to the front door of her home and went inside. With four other horses gone and without their income at the sale, she feared not being able to keep her farm going. After all, she was basically doing it on her own. But that's the way she liked it. Park had compared her to his American grandmother saying she was independent and stubborn. What was wrong with that? It was the American way, after all.

Park's rolling suitcase sat upright in the hallway. His canvas shoulder bag was propped against it. So he was leaving.

The smell of coffee wafted through the first floor of the house. She was hungry. She'd missed her morning coffee. Reggie walked through the dining room and into the kitchen. Just as she suspected, Park sat at the island, his back to her.

"I made coffee," he said without looking around.

"Thanks."

She avoided him by going to the other side of the island. Near the stove, she poured herself a cup of coffee. Then she opened the refrigerator for the carton of half-and-half. She also pulled out a piece of cold pizza wrapped in a plastic wrap.

"I'm starved," she said to make conversation. "Want a piece?"

"No. I had cereal."

Reggie bit off a piece of pizza and chewed it slowly. An outsider would never guess they'd spent the night engaged in wild sex. No one would guess the man sitting on the kitchen stool, nursing a mug of coffee, had only a few hours ago asked her to marry him.

She hardly believed it herself.

Park didn't say a word. What did she expect him to say? She took another bite of pizza. After swallowing it, she said, "Ben is outside if you want to go to Lexington."

He glanced at her. "Thanks. I want him to take me to Keeneland."

"Do you want me to tell him to wait?"

"No, I'm ready."

She nodded, suddenly realizing the finality of it all.

Park stood up and turned to her. His face was somber. There seemed to be a dull light in his eyes.

"Before I go," he said, "I want you to know I've inherited my American grandmother's estate. After you left the house, my mother called to tell me. She called to wish me happy birthday, but then she told me the news."

"That's wonderful, Park." She was genuinely happy for him.

"It means I'm no longer bound totally to my family."

What was he driving at? Did he think an inheritance would change things between them?

He took a step toward her. "In fact, I plan to go to Virginia to meet with my grandmother's lawyer. I've talked with him today by phone. I have property there now, Reggie. I can start my own farm. Breed my own horses."

"That's wonderful, Park," she repeated, unsure of what else to say.

"I'm resigning my position at the Stuart Racing Stable." His voice was firm. "My father and Hampton will have to get along without me."

Reggie couldn't believe Park was taking that action. "Are you sure?"

"As sure as anything I've ever done."

The surveyed each other. "I'm glad for you, Park."

"I have my grandmother's engagement ring in my pocket." He patted his pants pocket. "It's yours if you want it."

She shook her head, tension building within her. She couldn't marry him. She was afraid.

"But I'll not wait for long. I'm moving on with my life, Reggie, with or without you."

She nodded then. "I understand."

"We could make Ward Farm into a showplace," he said. "I have that kind of money. You wouldn't have to struggle. You wouldn't have to do it alone."

"But I'm used to doing it alone." Reggie raised her chin. "I don't need your help, Park."

"No, I guess you don't."

He left her then, going through the dining room. Reggie stood rooted in the spot, unable to move, hardly breathing. The door opened and shut. Park was gone.

Something told her she'd made a mistake. Something cried out that she was a fool. But then her stubborn side reminded her he hadn't said the "L" word when he was pleading his case. He didn't need her. He'd made himself clear. And she certainly didn't need him.

With her world collapsing around her, all Reggie wanted was a long, hot shower. She wanted to get out of yesterday's clothes. She wanted to wash the smell of sex from her body.

Just to make sure Park was really gone though, she traced his footsteps through the dining room and into the entrance hall. It was empty. No luggage. No Park. She glanced outside, and saw Ben's truck was gone.

For some damn reason, she started to cry slow burning tears. Turning to head upstairs, she spotted a sheet of paper on the side table near the stairs. It was Park's watercolor of Richlawn Hall. He'd left it for her.

That's when Reggie knew he'd also left her a little piece of his heart.

"Have you seen Park?" Reggie asked Ella, who was sitting behind her farm's welcome table like yesterday.

So much had happened since Reggie had sat beside her friend, doing the same job. It was incredible.

"No, why?"

"I need to talk to him." Reggie looked up to scour the area. The barn facility was packed with excited sale-goers much like yesterday.

"Reggie, what's wrong?"

Reggie glanced back at Ella. "Wrong? Nothing."

"You look different."

She stared at her friend knowing she felt different. Did it show? A night of lovemaking had changed her and so did losing her dream. That's what the Spiritmaker colt was. Her dream for the future. Now, she had nothing.

"There's Ben," Reggie said, noticing her farm manager lead a horse from its stall. "I'll catch up with you later."

Reggie scurried to catch up with Ben. She joined him in the parade around the walking path. A couple of buyers were watching. "Ben!"

"What are you doing here, Reggie?"

"I want to talk to Park. Where did you drop him off?"

Ben gave her a look she'd seen too many times before, one that he and her grandfather had given her when they thought she was doing something wrong. "What do you want with that guy?"

"He's leaving, and we didn't leave on good terms."

"Seems to me as if you were on great terms."

"Ben!"

"Just sayin'." The old man halted the horse and released a breath. "It's your business, Reggie."

"I know." She looked away, unable to meet his cautionary glance.

"That British guy cares for you, Reggie. He didn't say nothin' in the car, but I can tell."

She gazed at the man who was so much like a father. "Do you really think so?"

Ben nodded. "Corbin used to tell me this. If something isn't working out, you need to change the way you're doing it. 'Don't be afraid of change, Ben,' he'd say. That's all we have sometimes."

"What do you mean?"

"Think about it," Ben said. "Holding on to this farm isn't working out too well. Not with your dad throwing barriers in your path all the time. Maybe you need to change things."

"Like what?"

"I don't know. Just sayin'."

The yearling became restless and jerked on the lead line. Ben had a job to do. Reggie stepped aside and let him pass with the filly.

"Try the sales pavilion," Ben called over his shoulder. "He was going to meet his agent."

Reggie walked slowly through the barn area and out to the parking lot toward the pavilion. Ignoring all the activity around her, she was deep in her own head, thinking about what Ben had said. Ben was right. She didn't like change. When things changed, she no longer had control over them. Over herself. Controlling her life—her actions and reactions—was important to her. It made her feel secure. As if she knew what to expect from the day. From life.

But in the end, being in control of things was pure imagination. She hadn't been able to control that bolt of lightning. She couldn't control her wayward father. Her mother's cancer had been beyond her control too

Park said she ran away from things. That's because she was scared. But running away hadn't helped in the end. She still had to step up and face her problems. Take back control. Renew her hope.

Didn't Granddaddy always say without hope, a person has nothing?

Reggie stopped on the gravel and took a deep breath. The storm had washed away the heat and humidity. The sky was clear blue without a single cloud.

What was she scared of now? Losing Park? They were good

together, weren't they? And not just in bed. They had so much in common. They talked the language of horses. They had the same hopes and dreams—racing the next great horse, breeding the next Kentucky Derby winner.

Deep down—deep, deep down—she was scared of herself. She was afraid of opening up and letting other people see her. Was she frightened of what Park would find if he really knew her? Saw her the way she saw herself?

What if he didn't love her? Or stopped loving her?

That was something she couldn't control, wasn't it?

So what should she do? Run away again and lose hope? Or did she buck up and face her feelings for Parker Stuart the way she faced the daily challenges at the farm?

Without answering her questions, Reggie strode on, determined to find Park. She passed the van counter, where representatives from hauling companies met perspective clients, through the holding area, and out to the covered walking ring where the yearlings were led before going into the sales pavilion. Some sixth sense told her she'd find him there.

And she did. He and his agent were leaning against the railing overlooking the walking area. When she approached, the agent nodded and slipped away.

Reggie didn't say anything for a minute. She didn't know what to say. She'd never felt so helpless in her life. Glancing up, she surveyed Park's face. His gaze fell on the horses, as if he was ignoring her. His face was so familiar. So adorable. His eyes were focused on everything but her. Yet, she knew he was aware of her. Of her movement beside him. Of her closeness.

Gently, Reggie touched his thigh with her fingers. She felt a bulge in his jeans pocket.

"The engagement ring is still there," he said without looking down.

For that moment—maybe for only that moment—she had hope. It sprang within her like a flower in full bloom.

"I think I'd like to take the ring," she said.

He looked down his regal nose at her. "Think or know?"

She pulled herself up straight. She removed her sunglasses so he could see her eyes. Grinning up at him, she said, "I think I want to torment you, Parker Stuart, like your American grandmother tormented your poor, British grandfather."

"Ah, you said my given name."

"Maybe just this once," she conceded.

"You'll be forced to say it on our wedding day."

She cocked her head. "Okay, maybe I'll say it one more time."

Park turned to her then and caught her in his arms. "Do you love me?"

"Oh, that?" She toyed with him. "I've thought about it, and I'd have to say that the answer is 'yes.' What about you, sir?"

"I thought that was a given," he answered with a smile.

"Nothing is a given," Reggie said, philosophically.

"You're right, luv. If you'd asked me two hours ago whether I'd see you again, I would have answered no. But here you are."

Park placed a finger under her chin and lifted it. His kiss was sweet and held the promise of passion. Reggie answered him with a kiss, feeling for once as if this was right. This was hope. This was love. This was happiness.

When he broke off, Park gazed down at her and gave her another brilliant smile. "What do you say? Let's go buy Ward Farm a few young horses."

EPILOGUE

The February night was cold. Reggie and Park sat on bales of straw outside Spiritmaker's stall. The mare was showing signs of labor—heavy udders, dropped belly, and a lengthened vaginal opening. They were present to attend to the birth.

Excitement and anticipation rotated through Reggie's stomach, making her jittery. She couldn't stop her hands from shaking.

"Cold?" Park asked, grabbing a hand. "You need to put on your gloves."

"No, I'm not cold. Just nervous."

He nodded and put an arm around her shoulders, pulling her next to him.

"None of that now," Ben muttered, shuffling down the aisle with the foaling kit.

He sounded gruff, but Reggie knew he'd come around where Park was concerned. Their November wedding had proven Park's seriousness. That was good enough for old Ben. Now, Park was part of the family, and Ben treated him that way.

Ben entered the stall and ran a hand down the mare's back. Her head was low, and she was sweating. Juan had braided her tail earlier. Now, Ben put on a long, plastic sleeve to check whether the foal was in the right position.

Reggie and Park stood at the bars of the stall, watching Ben insert his hand.

"Nose first," Ben announced. "Head on the front legs. We're ready to go."

But Spiritmaker wasn't. Not quite yet. So Reggie and Park sat back down. For another hour, as her contractions increased, the mare circled her stall, agitated.

So much had happened in the months since the September sale. Park had been true to his word. That day at the sale, he had bought two yearlings, one for her and one for him, he said. The colt and the filly were living at Culpepper's until they were old enough to go into their two-year-old training. The horses were the foundation of their new, joint racing stable.

Much to the disapproval of his family, Park had quit his father's thoroughbred operation. Once his grandmother's estate was in his hands, Park sold the farmland but retained the house, because, as he told Reggie, he was too damn sentimental. After their marriage, he'd purchased land from Rod Culpepper, land that had once belonged to Reggie's grandfather. Now, they had room for expansion. Room to grow.

And Reggie was growing too. She placed a free hand on her belly and sighed softly. Already three months pregnant, she knew they hadn't wasted a bit of time during their wedding night.

Ben appeared once more and went into the stall. He put on another sleeve. This time when he checked the mare, her water broke, flooding the straw bedding.

"Show time!" Ben called.

Reggie and Park rushed to the stall. Through the bars, Reggie watched Spiritmaker lower herself to the ground. The mare grunted.

"You want to do the honors?" Ben asked Park.

"No, let Reggie."

Reggie stepped into the stall. The little legs were protruding. She grabbed hold of the tiny hooves and timing her pulls to each contraction, she helped the mare deliver her foal. With a huge sigh and a final push from the mare, the foal slipped into the world amid a flood of fluid, placenta, and blood.

"Oh, how beautiful!"

The wet foal blinked at the light.

"It's a colt," Park said. "Bright red like his brother."

Reggie thought of Jimmy and the hope she'd had for the horse. Hope that had died with him during that terrible storm.

But hope was an undying thing. It might come and go, but it was always available. It existed with the birth of a foal. It existed with every chance taken. It lived in the love Reggie felt for the man who looked at her through the bars of the stall. His look of love told her everything she needed to know. She didn't need to do it all alone. She didn't need to be afraid again.

"One thirty-two," Park said, glancing at his watch. He held out her leather binder. "Do you want to record the time of birth?"

"No," she said. "You do it. My hands are a bit messy."

As Park wrote in the time of birth, the little colt lunged to his feet, swaying unsteadily. Park recorded the time the foal stood. Then Spiritmaker heaved herself up and began to lick her baby clean. Reggie and the two men cleaned the stall, removing the afterbirth and wet straw and bringing in feed and fresh water. Then, as they watched, the foal wobbled toward his mother and began to nurse.

"We're done for the night," Ben said. "See you in the morning."

"S' long, Ben. Thanks again."

Reggie slipped her hand into Park's as they left the barn for the short walk to the house. The night had been wonderful. Nothing had gone wrong. Hopefully, Stuart Legacy's last crop would make its own legacy for her farm, hers and Park's.

"You know something?" Park gathered her into his arms when they reached the back porch. "Ben said we're done for the night. I'm not so sure about that."

Reggie lifted her face to him. In the yellow glare of the porch light, she gave him a wicked grin. "Something told me, Mr. Stuart, that you wouldn't be tired."

"You're so right, Mrs. Stuart." He kissed the top of her head. "I'm ready for a bottle of Guinness and a piece of cold pizza."

She put her arms around his neck. "Are you sure that's *all* you're ready for, luv?"

THE BLUEGRASS REUNION SERIES RETURNS!

Kentucky Woman

What is Jack willing to do to win the heart of this spirited Kentucky woman?

Kentucky Blue Bloods

When Kentucky blue blood tangles with British blue blood, are they willing to take a gamble on love?

Kentucky Bride / Kentucky Heat

Two novellas in one book

How far is Cam willing to go for his business? Can he turn a skittish Kentucky horse trainer into his Kentucky bride?

<>

Is Reggie crazy to think she can convince Hank he's more than just his daddy's name and fortune, without getting tangled up in his alluring Kentucky heat?

Kentucky Flame

Is there enough of an ember in the ashes of their past to reignite the flames of love?

Kentucky Groom

Can a marriage of convenience prove that a California millionaire can be the perfect Kentucky groom?

Kentucky Cowboy

Will Mandy take a second chance with her Kentucky cowboy and risk her heart this time?

Kentucky Rain

Carrying a torch is ridiculous. There's no time like the present to move on. But does Scott really want to?

Betting on Love

She fell in love with the first kiss.

Contemporary romances about second chances set in the Bluegrass of Kentucky that can be read as standalone novels with happily ever after endings and no cliffhangers

.

ABOUT THE AUTHOR

Whether it is the Bluegrass of Kentucky, the mountains of Montana, or Medieval England, Jan Scarbrough brings you home with romances from the heart.

Jan Scarbrough is the author of two popular Bluegrass series, writing heartwarming contemporary romances about home and family, single moms and children, and if the plot allows, about another passion—horses. Living in the horse country of Kentucky makes it easy for Jan to add small town, Southern charm to her books and the excitement of a Bluegrass horse race or a competitive horse show.

Leaving her contemporary voice behind, Jan has written paranormal gothic romances: Tangled Memories, a Romance Writers of America (RWA) Golden Heart finalist, and Timeless. Her medieval romance, My Lord Raven is a story of honor and betrayal.

A member of Novelist, Inc., Jan self-publishes her books with the help of her husband. She has published 25 romances.

Jan lives in Louisville, Kentucky, with two rescued dogs, one rescued cat, and a husband she rescued 21 years ago.

When she isn't writing, she loves to ride American Saddlebred horses, drive grandchildren to activities, and volunteer with Alley Cat Advocates. There is nothing she enjoys more than curling up with a good book.

Join Jan's mailing list at http://www.janscarbrough.com/ for news about new books and other possible appearances in your area. Follow Jan on Twitter @romancerider.

ALSO BY JAN SCARBROUGH

Bluegrass Homecoming Series

Prequel

Secrets

Nom de Plume

If you enjoyed Kentucky Blue Bloods, please consider reviewing it, and read Chapter One of Kentucky Bride at the end of this book.

Kentucky Bride / Kentucky Heat

Two novellas in one book

How far is Cam willing to go for his business? Can he turn a skittish Kentucky horse trainer into his Kentucky bride?

<>

Is Reggie crazy to think she can convince Hank he's more than just his daddy's name and fortune, without getting tangled up in his alluring Kentucky heat?

Sign up for my monthly newsletter mailing list and be the first to know about new books and giveaways just for newsletter subscribers. I promise your email address will never be shared.

Follow me on BookBub.

Visit me online any time at my website and my blog

THANK YOU!

For purchasing this book from
Saddle Horse Press